Fierce Resistance

Fiona Beddow is an ex-musician, teacher and author who writes adventure novels. When she is not hunched over a computer keyboard typing with four fingers, she works as a home tutor, specialising in helping children with special needs and building confidence in numeracy and literacy skills. She gives writing workshops with a musical twist, and talks to children about the adventure of writing. She is an advocate for the rights and aspirations of girls around the world.

Cover design: Spiffing Covers

Follow Fiona onTwitter
@FionaBeddow

www.fionabeddowbooks.com

FIERCE RESISTANCE

Fiona Beddow

PART ONE

Chapter One
Bittersweet

Two Malvanian soldiers stalked the pavement like crows looking for dead meat. Their black boots tapped out a robotic rhythm on the sun-baked concrete, and the sound drifted in through the bedroom window.

Beth Hardy lay on her bed with a large map spread in front of her. She sketched a line across it in pink felt pen, plotting her escape route to London. Beside her was a list of the items she needed to take with her, scribbled on the back of a chocolate wrapper.

There was a creak at the bottom of the stairs, and she heard the sound of her dad's feet padding towards her. She grabbed the list, folded the map into a bundle and stuffed them under the pillow, swapping them for an old copy of *Hey Girl!* magazine. Pushing a strand of pale brown hair behind her ear, she re-read her horoscope for nine weeks ago.

'Navy blue will be luck-luck-lucky for you!' chirped the snazzy purple writing, *'Wear it on Tuesday and watch that handsome hunk come running! And a weekend shopping trip will bring a fabulous bargain!'*

She shuddered. Whoever wrote that wasn't very good at predicting the future. A shopping trip, in *that* weekend of all weekends? And as for navy blue – it was now the most hated colour in the country.

Her dad's slippers scuffed on the carpet outside the door, and he knocked.

'How are you doing, Squidgy Bear?' He put his head round the door, smiled and came in. 'Thought you might like a bikky.'

Beth grinned and slid off the bed. 'I bet you didn't bring any Jammy Dodgers.' She took the plate of biscuits, picked up a Custard Cream and posted it into her dad's mouth.

'Thanks love,' he said. 'It's good to have something that makes life taste a bit sweeter…'

His voice faded to nothing. Outside, two pairs of highly polished army boots tick-tocked down the street.

'How's Mum?'

'Definitely having a bad day.'

Beth's skin crawled across her back like a damp slug. The unpleasant memories never stayed away for long. She nibbled through the crumbly outer layer of her biscuit into the chewy jam hiding in the middle, and the sugary strawberry soothed some of her heartache. She threaded her arm around her dad's waist and the two of them went over to the window.

Together they surveyed the street - the rose bush in the front garden, the moss on the front wall, and Mr Stone's brown car parked outside next door, with a dent in the side where it got hit by a motorbike. The sun was shining on the cherry tree at Mr Jafary's, and the stone statue of the angel at Mrs Hill's smiled peacefully. Beneath the angel's gaze, the two Malvanian soldiers prowled, each with a machine gun slung over his shoulder. One of them looked up. He patted the butt of his gun and smirked, the buttons on his navy blue uniform gleaming.

'Who's a pretty boy, then.' Her dad murmured through his teeth, in case the soldier could lip-read.

Beth gave him a squeeze. She looked away from the street in disgust and went downstairs, leaving her dad to keep watch on his own.

Her mum was sitting on the sofa in the living room, staring at the television, an uneaten chocolate biscuit slowly melting in her hand. A grinning clown called Smit leered from the TV screen. He sneaked up behind an old lady and smacked her round the head with a giant sausage. She collapsed on the floor and the TV audience laughed. The old lady didn't get up and Smit whacked her in the face.

Beth picked up the remote control.

'Why are you watching this, Mum?' she said.

She re-tuned to one of the *Information* channels. A man in a white coat appeared and a caption came up on the screen:

MASSEN PRÜDENTLISCH ELEKTRONIKAL - EKWIPMENT!
Use electronic equipment sensibly!

'Does he think we're all idiots?' said Beth.

Teardrops gathered on her mum's eyelashes, and the

bad memories haunted Beth again, twisting her insides into an ugly ball. She took hold of her mum's hand and her mum blinked slowly, releasing a cascade of plump tears down her cheeks.

'I'll make you a cuppa,' said Beth. She got up and left the room.

As the water fizzed and spluttered in the kettle she could still hear the man on the television telling her how to make a cup of tea. In a fit of rebellion, she unplugged the lead and tied several knots in it, tugging each one tight until it looked like a bizarre piece of modern sculpture. She plugged it back in and jabbed her finger at the mangled flex.

'What are you going to do about that, you Malvanian control freaks?' she hissed. 'Arrest me?'

The water rose to the boil and hot vapour gushed from the spout with a scream. She kicked the fridge door as hard as she could, ran out of the kitchen and fled upstairs into Peter's bedroom.

Everything was just as it had been for the past nine weeks. The Digby Digger duvet cover was smooth and untouched and big boxes of construction blocks stood unused on the shelf. Beth picked up a model of a fire engine that Peter had built. She flicked one of the wheels and made it spin round. Then she went over to the toy chest. There was a sign on the lid that had a drawing of a skull and crossbones on it and big green letters that said 'DO NOT OPEN TRESHER CHEST OR PIRITS WILL GET YOU'. She opened the lid, placed the fire engine inside, and took out Peter's book about cranes and trucks. He loved that book. He'd only got it for Christmas but already it was dog-eared and the cover was bent.

Peter's favourite teddy, Jackson, was lying on the pillow. Peter had taken him to bed with him every night since he was three months old, and seven years of cuddling had left him wilted and bald. Beth picked him up and ruffled his ears, and Jackson looked back at her with a wise and knowing look, as if he understood how she was feeling.

A huge pang of emotion exploded in her chest. She shut her eyes, screwed up her face and shook her head, trying to hold back all the terrible feelings that were threatening to flood through her body. But it was no use. Her legs gave way beneath her – and, clutching Jackson to her heart, she sat down hard on Peter's bed and began to cry her eyes out.

Chapter Two
Torn Apart

Nine weeks earlier, on the day before half term, Beth had arrived home from school feeling claustrophobic in her uniform. She ran upstairs, tugging at her tie and pulling the stiff collar away from her neck. She threw her schoolbag into a far corner of the bedroom and flopped backwards onto the bed.

As she stretched her hands and feet across the cool cotton of the duvet she heard Peter protesting from inside the bathroom.

'Why are you washing my hair? I can wash my own hair!'

She grinned. She'd seen the state of him the last time he'd washed it himself. He'd poured a whole bottle of shampoo on his head and his hair had dried into strange, foamy peaks like furry meringue.

'Owww!' Peter's voice echoed around the bath. 'You're rubbing too hard!'

She heard her mum say it was important to look nice when you go on a Beaver sleepover, and then there was a lot of splashing.

'I bet none of the other boys are being made to be clean!'

Her mum said that she bet that they were.

Beth laughed, removed her socks and tossed them across the room.

Then her mum said: 'I think we're going to have to sing the Washing Song.'

'No! That's for babies! I'm old now!'

'Wash, wash, washie, baby Peter's botty ...'

'You are just so embarrassing!'

'Come on, Peter! Join in! ... *Wash his fingers, wash his toes, wash his tiny baby nose ...*' Her mum dissolved into laughter. Peter was silent, and Beth knew he was scowling like a camel with a toffee stuck in its teeth.

'All right, you can wash my hair,' he said. 'But only for today.'

Beth put on the pink T-shirt she got for her thirteenth birthday and pushed her legs into a pair of size eight *petite* tracksuit bottoms. She applied lip gloss, flicked some mascara onto the long lashes that framed her chestnut-brown eyes, then skipped downstairs with bare feet. She found her dad standing watch over two steaming saucepans in the kitchen.

'Meatballs and spaghetti,' he said. It was Peter's favourite.

She hung on to his arm and nuzzled her cheek against the sleeve of his shirt. 'You didn't make this much fuss over me when I went away from home for the first time,' she said, trying to sound pathetic.

He kissed the top of her head.

'Oh, I think we *did*,' he said.

***

11

Peter ran along the landing in his underwear and shut himself in his room. He was in a bad mood. He looked at himself in the mirror, dug his fingers into his half-dry hair and ruffled it vigorously. His mum always made it look too smart and he hated it when it was all flat - but at least she didn't make him have girl's hair, like Dominic's mum did.

His Beaver uniform lay on the bed and as he put it on he began to feel like a little man again. He was a quick dresser, and was soon ready – but he had learnt that pretending to be slow gave him more time to play. He took a plastic steering wheel out of his toy box and climbed on to the bed. He sat on the bright yellow digger cab that was printed on the duvet cover, put the steering wheel in front of him and pretended to turn the ignition key. Jackson, his faithful teddy companion, sat beside him. The digger roared into life and he imagined lifting gigantic shovelfuls of rock high above the vehicle and transporting them - at great risk to himself - to a hydro-electric dam that was in danger of collapsing.

'Are you nearly ready, luvvie?' His mum was calling from downstairs.

'Not quite,' he called, putting the digger in reverse. His dinner would have to wait: water was leaking through a crack at the top of the dam and a catastrophic event was imminent. He dived off the bed; he and Jackson ran in slow motion to the other side of the room. He found a plastic screwdriver and struggled to the wardrobe, water already gushing down around him. Clinging on to a drawer knob, he used the screwdriver to open an imaginary sluice gate, and the water gushed away into

a special channel. The dam remained intact and millions
– no, *trillions* of lives were saved.

'Hurry up now, Peter!'

'I'm nearly ready!' He smoothed down his uniform
and wished that there was a Beaver badge for dangerous
digger driving.

'Good work, Jackson,' he said.

He sat on the edge of the bed and cradled the teddy
in his lap.

'You know I'm going to Beaver sleepover?'

Jackson definitely did.

'The thing is, the other boys won't have *their* teddies -
so you might get lonely.' He patted Jackson on the head.
'And Justin Baldwin says having teddies is dumb. So
you have to be brave and stay at home with Beth and
Mummy and Dad, OK?'

Jackson looked as if he understood perfectly. Peter
cuddled him and put him back on the pillow.

He ran downstairs, and when he arrived at the kitchen
doorway Beth was spooning some spaghetti into a
serving dish.

'Look at you!' she said. 'You're so clean you're almost
luminous!' Beth was funny. He wished he could think
of things to say like that. He also wished his skin could
actually glow in the dark.

'Photo time,' said his mum.

He posed for a photograph, standing up as straight as
he could, like a real soldier.

'Are you going to take Jackson with you?' she asked.

He said that - of course - he wasn't.

'Are you sure you'll be able to sleep without him?'

teased his dad.

Peter felt his cheeks go red – which was one of the worst feelings in the world. He curled his toes inside his socks and looked at the floor.

Beth patted him on the arm and gave him the salt and pepper.

'Why don't you take these into the dining room, Mr Super Scout?' she said.

Beth was cool. She always protected him from getting embarrassed.

'I'm not a scout, I'm a Beaver.'

'Super Beaver then, you wally!'

'I'm not a wally!'

'Yes you are. You ding-dong.'

***

At the scout hut, Beth got out of the car. She watched her mum straighten Peter's woggle and give him a goodbye hug; her dad ruffled his hair. Proudly, she flung her arms around him.

'You have a fantastic time, won't you? You can tell me all about it when you come home tomorrow night.'

She felt a twist in her heart, as if this separation was going to be too hard. On the day that Peter was born, she had looked at him in the carrycot and felt that her family was complete. He was the missing piece of the puzzle that she'd been looking for all those years when she had been an only child. Now, seven years later, she didn't want him to leave. She hugged him even more tightly, but this made tears well up in her eyes. So she let go, smiled valiantly and said, 'And remember to wash – I don't want to have a stinker for a brother!'

'You're not even funny,' grinned Peter, and he ran off.

As he climbed into the coach, Beth looked at her parents and she could see that they too were feeling the same wrench in their chests. She watched Peter walk up the aisle and sit down next to his friend Daniel Watson. The sun was setting and, as the coach pulled away, she waved goodbye. The last she saw of her brother was his little head of golden, curly hair bobbing up and down as he wriggled in his seat and laughed and joked with Daniel until the coach disappeared into the dusk.

The next morning she overslept. She went downstairs and discovered her parents standing in the living room, still wearing their pyjamas. Their faces were shocked and drawn. They were watching the twenty-four hour news on the television, which was showing rolling footage of a city being bombed.

'Where's this?' she asked.

Her dad could barely speak. 'It's London, sweetheart.'

On the television screen a huge explosion sent a dirty firework of masonry high into the air and terrified people ran for cover, trying to escape before the debris fell to the ground.

'The Houses of Parliament have been destroyed,' her dad said. 'They're saying other important buildings have been hit, too.'

A man limped towards the camera calling for help. His face was white with fear and dust, dark red blood oozing from his forehead.

'Who's doing it?' said Beth.

Both her parents shrugged.

'And why isn't our army fighting back?'

Her mum didn't take her eyes off the television. 'We barely have an army anymore,' she said.

'The soldiers we do have left are fighting wars in other countries,' her dad said bitterly. 'Ruddy government. They were warned about defence cuts. Didn't listen.'

A caption saying 'BREAKING NEWS' passed along the bottom of the screen. The newsreader confirmed that government buildings in Birmingham, Manchester, Liverpool and Cardiff had also been destroyed. New footage of devastation and damage appeared on the screen: shots of smoking rubble and ambulances speeding past; foreign soldiers beating up civilians; news reporters flinching as the streets cracked open behind them. And then the TV screen went blank. When the picture returned, the British newsreader had gone. In his place sat a large man in an old-fashioned navy blue uniform.

'People of Britain...' His accent sounded European. 'The Malvanian army has taken control of your country. We have captured your Prime Minister. We have taken your Queen. Our troops will soon arrive in your towns and cities. If you welcome us, you will be unharmed. If you resist us, you will be punished.'

The man saluted and military music started playing in the background. The newsroom faded out, and a film began, showing luscious countryside under a cloudless sky. Hundreds of dancing children appeared and skipped through the fields - happy children with fresh, clean faces, holding hands and smiling in their smart navy blue uniforms. A little boy with blond hair waved the Malvanian flag, and the camera zoomed in on it. The billowing fabric filled the screen, bearing the image of an outstretched eagle in navy blue on a white background. It was carrying a huge sword in its wings, and its talons were buried deep in a map of the world.

The appearance of the little blond boy reminded Beth of Peter. Her mum screamed his name and rushed to snatch the telephone from its base. She tried to dial the Scout Leader's mobile phone number, but kept hitting the wrong buttons.

Her dad intervened. 'Let me.'

Beth watched him key in the digits, then look puzzled. He gave the phone a tap and returned it to his ear. He pressed a few more buttons, shook the handset and listened again. Then he shrugged helplessly.

'The phone's gone dead.'

Chapter Three
Betrayal

After hours of being glued to their television sets and radios, wide-eyed and shell-shocked people wandered out of their homes, huddling together to gossip in the street. Beth walked to the front gate to get some air. Mr Jafary was on the other side of the road, talking to Mrs Hill, who was making flustered gestures with an empty carrier bag.

'The newsagent's is closed!' shouted Mr Jafary. 'No British news today, it's not allowed! They have taken the papers away so we can't find out the truth!'

Mrs Hill carried on twittering.

'And poor Mrs Hill couldn't buy any peppermints because the shop is shut!' said Mr Jafary.

Beth didn't care about Mrs Hill's mints. She looked along the street. Two little boys were running round in circles in their front garden, playing at being Malvanians and shooting each other with plastic water pistols. Her dad came out in his slippers and touched her on the arm.

'There's going to be an announcement,' he said, gesturing for everybody to come inside the house.

Her mum and Mr and Mrs Stone were already inside,

watching a repeat of the propaganda film with the smiling, dancing children. As she sat down on the sofa next to Mr Jafary, the film was interrupted by a loud military fanfare - and the face of the Malvanian General appeared in close-up, his steel-grey eyes staring from underneath a pair of thick, black eyebrows.

I hate him, thought Beth.

'People of the Island Republic of Malvania,' said the General from the TV screen. 'I have very bad news.'

'Someone's told him how ugly he is,' said her dad.

The General continued. 'Your Queen has refused to obey us. The Royal Family shall be put in prison and they will remain there until they decide to co-operate.'

There was film footage of the Queen being pushed into a van; the Prince of Wales was taken away in handcuffs. Mrs Hill began to cry into a lace hanky.

'God save the Queen!' said Mr Jafary.

Another fanfare blared into the living room and the programme cut back to the TV studio.

'Look, there's the Prime Minister!' squeaked Mrs Hill.

The Prime Minister gave a fake smile from a black leather armchair. 'These are dark and difficult times. It is my job to put Britain, and the people of Britain, first.'

The camera pulled back. He was sitting at a carved wooden desk, holding an embellished gold fountain pen, and the Malvanian General was standing over him.

'That is why I have signed this treaty with the Malvanians,' he said. 'I truly believe this is a positive step for Britain.'

He made a short speech, promising that becoming part of the Malvanian Empire would 'make Britain better'. He announced that he would be moving into Buckingham Palace to take up his new post as the General's Assistant. He wished everybody prosperity and happiness - and then, in a final act of betrayal, he stood up and kissed the General on both cheeks. Then he smiled at the camera again.

That night, Beth watched miserably as her parents paced in front of the television, keeping themselves awake so they didn't miss any important news. But at three o'clock in the morning, she finally withdrew to her room. Her whole body ached with worry for Peter, and she could not bear to see her parents so unhappy.

She left the curtains open and lay on her duvet. Outside, little squares of light peppered the view - it seemed that, in every house, somebody was still awake. Her fatigued muscles slowly melted into the bed and, after a while, the lighted windows seemed to swirl around each other. Her eyelids flickered and drooped and she sank into sleep.

She woke, shivering, two hours later. As she turned to crawl under the bedcovers she heard shouting outside, and a lorry rumbling into the street. She dragged herself upright and went to the window, scooping up the duvet and draping it over her shoulders. A Malvanian soldier jumped off the back of the truck and began patrolling the pavement, and as he walked past the house he saluted someone. Beth looked down and saw Mr Stone standing by his front gate, returning the salute and standing to attention. Suddenly she felt hungry, and headed downstairs.

Her parents were asleep on the sofa with a blanket

drawn up over their legs. The television was still on with the volume turned down. She switched it off and went into the kitchen. She shuffled from cupboard to cupboard, wearing her duvet like a cloak, preparing breakfast with one hand and holding the duvet with the other, too tired to go any faster – and, eventually, it was ready.

'Something smells good!'

Her dad seemed a bit better after his sleep. He helped himself to a large bite of toast and gave her a kiss, and as Beth wiped a smear of butter from her cheek there was a knock at the door.

'Who do you reckon?' said her dad. He was trying to sound cheerful. 'Maybe the Malvanian General wants to borrow the lawnmower. For his eyebrows.'

It was Daniel Watson's parents.

'We came round straight away,' said Mr Watson. 'We didn't know who else to talk to. What do you think of the news?'

'What's happened?' said Beth.

'Haven't you seen the announcement?'

Beth shrank into the duvet cloak and tried to look inconspicuous. Why had she switched the television off? She watched her dad steady himself against the radiator, in anticipation of bad news. Her mum hurried into the hall. She was biting her lip. A tiny spot of white appeared where the tooth touched the skin.

'It's OK,' said Mrs Watson. 'They're safe.'

The whiteness from her mum's lip seemed to spread over her entire body. Her knees buckled and she dropped onto the bottom stair.

'They've released a new propaganda film,' said Mrs Watson.

'With British kids this time,' said Mr Watson. 'They said that all missing children are being looked after in special Malvanian Youth camps. They will receive an elite education and have lots of wonderful opportunities not provided by the British education system.'

For a while nobody spoke, and Beth fidgeted under the duvet.

'Is that good?' she said.

Mr Watson shrugged.

'It's good,' said her dad, but his eyes said different. He took her mum by the hand and helped her to stand up. 'Perhaps we'll all feel a bit better after we've had some breakfast.'

The two families shared what Beth had cooked, with extra bacon and scrambled eggs made by Mr Watson. Beth listened as the adults talked in low voices, trying to comfort themselves with stories about the mischief their sons got up to together. But her mum spoke and ate very little, and Beth had never seen her look as fragile; like a tissue paper version of her normal self.

They were interrupted by another knock at the door. It was Mr Stone.

'I heard the news - you must be so pleased,' he said. 'Phyllis has sent me round with some muffins.'

Her dad attempted a smile. 'Well, tell Phyllis thank you very much,' he said. 'We're just thankful that the boys are safe.'

'But you must be glad that your boys have such an opportunity,' continued Mr Stone, his eyes gleaming behind the lenses of his steel-rimmed spectacles. 'A Malvanian education is a very sought-after thing, you know. It's a marvellous country - I've always thought so.'

Beth flinched as her dad banged his fist on the table.

'How dare you!' he said.

'I think you should leave,' said Mr Watson.

'I was just saying, some good can come out of this! A bit of discipline might stop all this anti-social behaviour…'

The two fathers grabbed Mr Stone by the elbows and took him to the front door. Beth stared at the crumbs on her plate and listened - there was a scuffle in the hallway, then the front door opened and slammed shut again. She remembered Mr Stone's salute after the soldier had got off the lorry and a shiver ran down her back. The enemy was everywhere.

Chapter Four
Going Places

Peter looked eagerly out of the coach window. The Malvanian soldiers had promised them a big adventure before bedtime, and it was starting to get dark.

The soldier who was travelling with them had a shiny metal gun, and it looked like a real one, which was very exciting. The coach turned a corner and Peter could tell from the sound of the engine that it was going to stop. The other boys sensed it too and a ripple of chatter broke the sleepy silence. Peter nudged Daniel awake and, as they pressed their faces against the glass, the coach glided across a vast car park and came to a halt in front of the biggest toy megastore Peter had ever seen.

He counted six other coaches parked there. Twelve soldiers were guarding the shop, their machine guns big and black with dozens of golden bullets gleaming from each belt. Beneath the brightly lit shop sign, the entrance doors slid open and a group of children came out. Somebody let out a whoop of excitement and everybody rushed to one side of the coach to get a better look. Peter couldn't believe his eyes: each child was carrying a brand new toy.

A lady in a smart white dress got on the coach and wrote everybody's name on a clipboard.

'You vill follow me,' she said. She seemed nice, and she led them across the car park and into the store.

'Look children - what lovely toys,' she said. 'Come and choose your favourite!'

They were allowed to play with as many things as they liked, and Peter ran from one toy display to another. He picked up two diggers, a space gun and several boxes of construction blocks, which made his arms ache, so he knelt down and tried out a digger and the space gun. Daniel had chosen a cuddly stegosaurus. Soon everyone was in groups, sitting on the floor to play. Then a host of ladies in white dresses came in through a door, tidied up the mess of discarded toys and disappeared again without a sound.

The nice lady clapped her hands. 'You vill come,' she said. 'And bring your chosen toy with you.'

She took them into a large back room, where another coach party of children were waiting for them, surrounded by more of the nice ladies.

'Velcome,' said a tall woman with shiny hair. 'Sit.'

She told them that they would be allowed to take their toys away with them.

'But first,' she said, 'you must learn a special song.' She picked up a guitar and asked the children to copy her, line by line.

'It's called ze *Question Song*.'

She strummed the introduction.

'Don't ask questions;
Question marks are bad.
Children who ask questions
Are sad and wrong and mad.
'Which?' and 'When?' and 'Where?' and 'Who?'
Are words you mustn't try,
'What?' and 'How?' are naughty too -
But the worst of them all is 'Why?' '

Peter wasn't sure about this song. He liked asking questions, because life was interesting and complicated and puzzling. But no-one else seemed to mind singing it - and anyway, he wanted to be allowed to keep his super blaster gun, so he joined in loudly.

The lady stopped playing and pointed to an older boy sitting on the opposite side of the room. He had short, bristly hair and a silver earring in one ear.

'You are not singing,' said the lady.

'I hate singing,' said the boy. 'And yer song's rubbish.'

Peter quietly rubbed his hands together. He wished he could say things like that.

One of the lady's eyebrows rose slightly. 'I am sorry to hear you speak zis way,' she said.

She walked to the side of the room, opened up a small silver case and took out a syringe with some yellow liquid in it. Two other ladies stepped forward, took hold of the boy and pulled him to his feet, twisting his arms behind his back. The lady with the shiny hair pushed the needle into the boy's neck, squeezing it until the yellow liquid disappeared.

For a moment, the boy's eyeballs looked as if they were

going to burst out of his head. His mouth distorted into a horrible shape; his body went stiff like a scarecrow. Then he relaxed again and the two ladies lowered him to the floor. The shiny-haired lady returned to the front. She disposed of the syringe and straightened the collar on her clean, white dress.

'Everyone in zis room vill sing nicely,' she smiled.

The music started up again. Peter tried to sing with his best voice, but it was difficult because his throat felt as if there was something stuck in it. He began to think he would rather go home than have a new space gun. Daniel was cuddling his stegosaurus and staring at the older boy. Peter prodded him and sang as brightly he could, desperately willing Daniel to join in before anyone noticed.

The injected boy sang contentedly, rocking himself backwards and forwards in time to the music, his eyes lolling about in their sockets. The verse came to an end and the lady with the shiny hair shouted 'Repeat!'

The boy gave a lop-sided grin. *'Don't ask questions,'* he sang, and dribbled on his T-shirt.

Later, the children lined up at the exit with their toys. Daniel had started to cry, and Peter fidgeted nervously. A man in a suit came in and spoke to one of the ladies in white dresses – and now he was pointing at Daniel. Peter touched him on the arm and whispered 'Ssshh,' and the man pointed at him too and he was sure they were both going to get an injection. And then the man came over.

'What is the problem with zis child?' he asked.

Peter decided the safest thing was not to answer, and looked at his feet.

'No matter,' said the man. 'A quick wash of ze face and he won't look so bad. He is a handsome boy.'

As Peter studied his shoelaces, a sweaty hand grabbed him by the chin and tweaked his head upwards. The man's face was so close that Peter could see the little black pores on his nose. I will not cry, he thought. *I will not cry.*

'Very cute,' said the man. 'Very cute indeed.'

He gestured to the lady in white, and she nodded.

'You two vill come with me,' he said.

Daniel sobbed loudly. The man led them out of a side door where another coach was waiting. It had an upstairs and big, comfy seats. The man indicated that they should climb aboard.

'Congratulations,' he said. 'You are very lucky children.'

Peter didn't want to be lucky. He wanted to get on a bus that would take him home.

The man smiled and showed a row of very shiny teeth. Peter's jaw ached as he tried to hold back his tears.

'Your mummies and daddies vill be very proud of you,' said the man.

A soldier stepped down from the bus and patted both boys on the head.

'Don't look so sad - you are going to be on ze television.'

Peter and Daniel were helped inside. The doors swished closed, the engine throbbed and the coach accelerated away from the brightly lit car park and into the dark streets beyond.

Chapter Five
Normal but Not Normal

'This Malvanian stuff is such a drag,' said Beth's friend Melissa.

They were walking along the corridor on the first day of school after the summer half term.

The door to the History room was open; Beth looked in and saw a new, young teacher standing by the desk at the front, jangling his keys nervously in his pockets.

'Where's Mr Dyche?' she said.

Melissa shrugged.

They entered their classroom where Mrs Green was waiting for them. She handed out new timetables.

Melissa sighed noisily. 'Oh Lord, what's this?' she said. 'Malvanian History, Malvanian Geography, Malvanian Politics! No French, no German, no Spanish…Where's all the normal stuff?'

'Excuse me, Miss,' said Beth, 'does this mean we're going to have Malvanian lessons?'

Mrs Green said that only members of the Youth Movement were allowed to speak Malvanian.

'Hurrah!' said Melissa.

Mrs Green frowned. 'Open your maths books and get started. In silence, please.'

'Er, Miss?'

Beth covered her face with her hands. She couldn't believe Melissa's behaviour sometimes.

'Why wasn't Miss Fullager in assembly?'

'I'm afraid that...' Mrs Green's voice wavered. 'I'm afraid that Miss Fullager was arrested for distributing anti-Malvanian leaflets and taken away. In a '*Komplianz*' van.'

'Compliance, Miss?'

'It's the Malvanian private police force.' Mrs Green fiddled nervously with her necklace. 'But ... I'm sure Miss Fullager will be all right.'

The girl sitting behind Beth whispered that the *Komplianz* van drivers injected people - and turned them into zombies who could be made to do anything the Malvanians wanted. Melissa, who could never resist a good horror story, laughed and blurted it out in front of everyone.

'Really, what nonsense ...'

The colour seemed to drain out of Mrs Green's face, leaving her make-up prominent on her skin. She tugged harder at the necklace; it snapped and fell to the floor. 'That's enough now.' She bent down and picked up the broken silver chain. 'No more questions.'

'Maybe tomorrow I could ask her where Mr Dyche has gone,' murmured Melissa.

'Don't you dare,' said Beth.

The lesson passed in silence and, after the bell went and Mrs Green had left the room, Beth kicked Melissa's chair.

'You and your big mouth.'

'What? The Malvanians are rubbish!' said Melissa.

'They'll have piddled off home in three weeks – just you wait!'

***

Three weeks later, Beth was sitting in the garden with her dad in the mid-June sunshine, sharing a bar of Malvanian chocolate. British chocolate had been banned. Her dad waved the last square of '*Froöt ind Nutz*' in the air before putting it into his mouth.

'I must admit, it's very tasty,' he said, 'even if it does come from a dubious source.'

Mr Stone's face appeared over the garden fence and her dad's expression darkened.

'Talking of 'dubious',' he said.

'A happy afternoon to all you citizens,' said Stone, nodding towards the empty wrapper on the patio table. 'Best chocolate in the world, that is.' His spectacles gleamed in the sunlight, making him look as if he had shiny, yellow eyes like a robot.

'We were just going indoors - weren't we, Beth?'

But Mr Stone hadn't finished.

'I was just thinking how beautifully tidy the streets are these days. Had you noticed? Not a scrap of litter anywhere. Wasn't like that before, was it? It just goes to show what the right sort of rules can do, if they're done in the right way.'

As her dad stood up and marched indoors, Beth screwed the chocolate wrapper into a ball and imagined throwing it at Mr Stone's head.

'You should join the Malvanian Youth, my dear. They're always recruiting, did you know that? In fact I picked up an application form, in case you were tempted. I'm sure you don't want to miss out on the education that young Peter is having.'

Beth's head pounded with indignation. She stared at Mr Stone, blinking furiously for several seconds before turning and striding into the house.

Her dad was slumped on the sofa, the TV remote in his hand. He looked defeated.

'Your silly old dad tried to put the cricket on,' he said.

All cricket matches had been cancelled. The Malvanian government said it was 'too British' and had to be eliminated. The new summer sport was *Flünken*, a non-competitive game where two '*flünkers*' or 'servers' shot yellow discs out of a cannon, and the players had to try and catch them in square-shaped nets. The Malvanian Youth were being trained to play it.

'Let me know if anything good comes on,' said her dad, handing her the remote control. 'I think I'll walk up to the bus stop and meet your mum. Ta-ta, love.' He gave Beth a kiss and left the room.

She sat down and flicked through the channels. Health and safety programme … … the General … … Smit the clown… … the General … … the General's Assistant speaking from his new office at Buckingham Palace (Beth made a rude gesture at the television) … … health and safety … … the General … … the Malvanian Youth at *Flünken* training … …

She laughed to herself; it was such a rubbish game. All those poor kids with their stupid nets and all that ridiculous safety equipment; it's like hockey for idiots …

A new, unexpected image flashed across the screen.

She choked on her own breath, scrambling across the floor in such ferocious haste that she grazed her knees on the carpet. She squinted at the television, waiting for another close-up of the younger children at training.

'Come on, come *on*!' she said, tapping the glass, trying to make the picture change more quickly. Finally a group of seven year-olds huddled round the camera – and, peering out from under one of the helmets, was Peter. Hot tears spilled down Beth's cheeks and she touched the screen again, caressing Peter's face.

'I love you *so* much!' she said. 'You're my bestest brother ever, you know that, don't you?'

Just at that moment Peter smiled, and Beth closed her eyes and imagined giving him the biggest cuddle, his little golden head resting on her shoulder. When she opened her eyes again a split second later the camera had gone to a 'long' shot. Peter had disappeared into the crowd, and her heart howled with grief inside her.

She was about to turn off the television when she recognised the red-brick building in the background. It was a famous private school in London.

'I cannot leave him there on his own!'

She jumped up and scraped her hair off her face with both hands, as if exposing her forehead would help her think more clearly. An idea was forming in her head that made her heart quicken and her mouth taste of sweat.

Was she really going to do this? Mum was already in bits because of Peter, and the other day she was sure she'd heard Dad crying in the bathroom. She chewed her nails until she bit into her skin and it hurt.

The pain seemed to focus her. She walked out through the back door, down the garden path and out through the gate. She let herself into the Stones' back yard, approached the back door and knocked. Mr Stone's shiny face welcomed her. Beth greeted him, then fixed her face into a sweet smile:

'Can I have that Malvanian Youth application form? I think I would like to join after all.'

Chapter Six
Getting Ready

Beth rang Melissa's doorbell for the third time.

'Come on, Melissa – it's urgent.'

The front door opened slightly and Melissa's voice reverberated through the crack.

'Patience is a virtue, don't-you-know!' She was trying to sound posh.

'I really need to talk.'

'You can't come in unless you close your eyes first.'

It was no use arguing. Melissa let go of the door and Beth heard her run upstairs and shut herself in the bathroom.

'Now go and wait in my room!' she yelled.

Beth walked up slowly and sat on the edge of Melissa's bed, looking out of the window. After twenty minutes, to stop herself going mad with waiting, she picked up a little silver-framed mirror, swept her hair off her face and secured it with a pretty clip. She applied a layer of *Candy Phlox* lipstick, pressed her lips together and looked at herself from different angles. She looked nice, she thought.

The bedroom door burst open and Melissa flounced in.

'Ta-da! What do you think, darling?'

She had swathed herself in the longest and fluffiest pink feather boa that Beth had ever seen. Feathers poked out of her hair in all directions. She was wearing purple lipstick and enormous false eyelashes, which she fluttered ridiculously, and she had far too much blusher on.

'Do I not look marvellous?'

Beth couldn't remember the last time she had laughed so much.

'You look like a disco chicken! ... Oh God!' she said, bending double to try and ease the stitch in her stomach, 'take those eyelashes off before I die!'

Melissa flopped next to her.

'What colour is that lipstick?' said Beth.

'*Mauve Marshmallow.*'

'It's awful!'

Outside the window two Malvanian soldiers crossed past each other.

'That one with the brown hair is so *gorgeous*,' said Melissa.

'I suppose ...' said Beth. She had been watching the soldiers while Melissa was in the bathroom, and now they were walking away from each other, one towards the bottom of the road and the other back towards the Malvanian checkpoint in the next street.

'They cross over exactly every two and a half minutes, did you know that?' she said.

'Flippin' Nora, you are such a nerd sometimes! Who cares about that?' said Melissa.

'And there's a fifteen second gap when there are no soldiers in the street at all.'

Melissa gave her an odd look, then turned to

watch the brown-haired soldier as he disappeared round the corner.

'He looks even better from behind,' she purred.

Beth hadn't noticed.

'Do you know anyone who has got across the *Kantonlein* checkpoint, the one round the corner from here?'

'Bernie Jones has to cross it every day,' said Melissa. 'He has a special pass.'

The brown-haired soldier reappeared and walked back along the pavement towards them. Melissa craned her neck out of the window and waved.

'Coo-ee!' she squawked, 'I like your sexy trousers!'

The soldier was startled. Not surprisingly, thought Beth: Melissa looked like a Barbie who'd spent the night in a dustbin.

'No – I mean, has anybody tried to cross the *Kantonlein* without a pass?'

Melissa blew the soldier a kiss, which he ignored. She turned round in a huff.

'Of course no-one's tried! They shoot people who do.'

'Do you think there are many soldiers out in the countryside?'

Melissa flicked one end of the boa against the window frame. 'What's with all the weirdo questions?' she said.

The soldiers had disappeared again. Beth turned away from the window and grabbed Melissa's hand.

'I have to get to London, and I really need you to help me.'

***

ATTENTION!
THESE FOODS ARE NOW BANNED FROM
SCHOOL LUNCH BOXES:
Traditional style sandwiches
Scones, crumpets, Chelsea buns,
Victoria sponge, Eccles cakes etc
Cornish pasties, Cumberland sausages,
ploughman's lunches
Trifles, apple pies
Fish 'n' chip & roast dinner flavour crisps

BANNED ITEMS WILL BE CONFISCATED. GIRLS
BREAKING THE RULES WILL BE DEALT WITH.
Patricia Macleod, Headteacher.

Beth waited whilst Mrs Macleod checked her lunch. Her stomach tightened: hidden in her ham roll was a dab of English mustard.

The Headteacher gave the lunch a nod of approval and Beth turned to see Melissa waving at her from the far corner of the dining hall. Melissa had taken steps to ensure the two of them could talk undisturbed: she had pushed the surrounding tables further away and removed any spare chairs. A girl approached and asked Melissa if she could sit with her; Melissa stuck her tongue between her lower lip and teeth and acted as if she were demented, and the girl hurried away. Melissa continued to enjoy herself, flapping her arms like a lunatic, until Beth sat down beside her.

'What did you do with all the chairs?'
'Look!'

Extra girls were sitting at the nearest tables, crammed elbow to elbow and chatting loudly.

'No-one will hear us talking now.' Melissa was taking this very seriously. She unwrapped a baguette and spoke with her mouth full.

'I have appointed myself Co-Commander of 'Operation Brother Rescue'.' She swallowed eagerly and glanced around the room. 'It's amazing that you're doing this.'

Beth leant back in her chair and picked at the ham roll. As soon as she thought about Peter her appetite always left her.

'Cheer up - I've worked out where you can stay on the first night of your journey. Remember the old hut? You could easily get there in one night.'

This was an excellent plan. Five years ago, Melissa had got one of her mad ideas, and persuaded Beth to set out across the fields at the outskirts of town in search of adventure. Fuelled by an unhealthy mixture of cola and Kendal mint cake, the two girls had walked for miles until they saw a small copse in the middle distance. They ran towards it, then flitted between the trees, finally discovering an old charcoal burners' hut in a clearing. The roof was half missing and the windows were cracked and dirty, and a rusty brazier stood outside, full of leaves and choked by nettles. Inside were a table, chairs and the remains of a bunk bed. The hut became their secret camp and they returned every summer, thrilling in the belief that they were the only people who knew it was there.

'It's a brilliant idea,' said Beth.

The smoky ham and crusty bread smelled appealing again, and she began to eat.

'It's perfect.'

Melissa chewed noisily and grinned.

That afternoon, the lessons passed quickly, and Beth's head was still spinning with plans on the bus journey home. When she got off at her stop she noticed that a new set of recycling containers had been delivered to every house. There were eleven different bins. One of them said:

> 'NOR GREENEN VEGETABALEN.
> KAROOTZEN VERBIDDEN.
> Green Vegetables only. No carrots.'

Another read:

> 'PLASTICK-BOTTLE-TOPPEN.'

She glanced up and down the street, then smashed her foot into a square yellow bucket that said 'Clothes But Not Socks'. With a clamour it bounced across the pavement and landed in the gutter, and she continued on her way.

About ten metres further down the street she heard a vehicle driving slowly towards her from behind. A large white van drew level with her and the uniformed driver wound down the window and leant out.

'Naughty, naughty,' he said.

With a sharp turn of the steering wheel, he revved the engine and drove onto the pavement, blocking her path.

'You are going to wish you hadn't kicked that bucket.'

He got out and opened the rear door of the van. It was immaculately clean and a single word was written on it in dark blue:

Komplianz

Chapter Seven
Isolation

The driver pushed Beth into the back of the van. He climbed in after her, closed the door and removed a pair of handcuffs from his belt. In a single movement he snapped the cuff around one of her wrists, swung her upwards and shackled her to a clip above her head. She reeled: the van was white inside from top to bottom and for a moment she didn't know whether she was the right way up.

The driver smiled.

'My English is very good, don't you think?'

Beth shrugged.

The Malvanian smiled again. He raised his hand to her cheek and gave it a gentle pat. 'You are a sweet girl,' he said.

He moved towards a silver storage box at the front of the van and returned with a syringe and a small vial full of yellow liquid. Still smirking, he filled the syringe from the vial. He pressed the needle into the skin on her neck.

'I will say it again.' His breath was right in her face. 'My English is very good, don't you think?'

Beth gave a slight nod; any sudden movement would send the needle shearing into a vein.

'Not good enough,' sneered the Malvanian. 'Say it: *'Your English is very good'.*'

She heard a tiny voice come from her throat:

'Your English is very good.'

He continued. *'And I am very impressed.'*

'And I … am very impressed.'

'In future, I will do as I am told. Because if I don't, a nice Komplianz man will come to my house with his medicine…' He applied more pressure to the needle, taking her skin to breaking point. *'… And everyone in my family will be punished because I have been a naughty girl.'*

She got the words out somehow. The driver climbed out, closed the door behind him and started up the engine. The van made an abrupt reverse turn that sent her smashing into the side wall. Then it shot forward, and for a moment she felt weightless, suspended by the handcuffs, before she fell back again. The driver drove at reckless speed; then the van spun round one hundred and eighty degrees, sending her, flailing and helpless, face first into the wall. She let out a yell and he stopped the van. The engine fell silent; she could hear a song playing on the radio in the driver's cab and realised that her heart was beating twice as fast as the music.

The lights went off. The engine kicked back into life and they drove round and round in circles, Beth spinning like a corkscrew, the handcuffs cutting deeper into her wrist with every turn, her shoulder burning with pain. After a sudden stop and a long pause, the van set off again, swerving this way and that, her body taking a battering despite her attempts to cushion the impact with her free arm.

Finally they came to a screeching halt. The door opened and the driver released her. She was back by the recycling buckets.

'Now pick that up,' said the driver.

Beth lifted the yellow bucket out of the gutter and returned it to the pavement.

'No. Put it exactly where you found it.'

She hesitated, and the driver sneered. 'I think you'll find it was one-and-a-half centimetres to the left.'

A curtain twitched in the house opposite, and Beth made the final, humiliating adjustment.

'Remember what I said about your family.' The driver got back in his van, gave two clicks of his tongue and sped away.

Beth found a handkerchief in her schoolbag and cleaned up her face. She took her phone out of her pocket and tried to send a text to Melissa, but her brain would not focus.

Slens
No …

Psals
No, wait …

Plan's non
She started to cry. Why was she being so useless?
She gritted her teeth.

Plan's off.

She wiped her eyes and turned the corner into her

43

street. She could see her dad tending the rose bush in the front garden. He saw her, his face lit up and he waved.

She pulled her shirt sleeve down to hide the cuts on her wrist, bit the inside of her cheek hard and texted Melissa again.

I can't do it.

***

Peter sat in the Study Room doing his Malvanian homework. He chewed his pencil, trying to remember the Malvanian for '*I am happy*'. At the next table, a group of girls were fussing over Daniel. Girls always did that to Daniel for some reason - but it was good because it stopped Daniel crying all the time. This was important, because if you behaved well and didn't get noticed, then the adults wouldn't hurt you.

He sneaked a guilty glance at the silver 'medicine' case on the table, and a feeling of terror came over him, making him want to go to the toilet. He asked the Matron if he could be excused, and she smiled.

'Again, Peter? You have a very excitable bladder. We vill have to call you 'Peter-ze-Pee-Pee'.'

Matron was right: he did want to pee a lot these days.

After he had locked himself in the toilet cubicle he reached out to the sides and touched the walls. He liked coming in here: he didn't feel as lonely when he was hiding somewhere that was only big enough for one person.

When he had finished he put the toilet lid down and

sat on it, listening to make sure no-one else was in the bathroom. Satisfied that he was alone, he reached into his shorts pocket and took out the teaspoon that he had stolen at lunchtime. At the sight of it, his stomach somersaulted in horror, and for a moment he considered flushing the spoon away before he could be caught and punished. But he turned it over in his hands, feeling the curves of the metal between his fingers, and imagining the power and heat that had gone into manufacturing it. He remembered how much he hated the Malvanians, and pictured himself heroically using the teaspoon to dig a tunnel. He would burrow underneath the school field into a nearby garden, where he would crawl out under a bush and make his escape - just like in the movies.

He hadn't decided where to start the tunnel yet. He knew it had to be in a room with mud under the floorboards, and he wasn't sure where he could find one of those. He understood it would take a long time to dig (maybe three whole weeks) and, of course, there would have to be a back-up tunnel … but he was confident he could do it, if only he could get started.

Better still, Mum or Dad or Beth might have seen him on TV and were coming to rescue him. He jiggled his legs backwards and forwards and wondered which one of them would come to take him home. It could be Daddy, because Daddy didn't like nasty people like the Malvanians bossing him around - but Daddy had to go to work and get money for things, so maybe he was too busy right now. He was sure Mummy would want to come and get him, because of how much she loved him - but she might get scared, especially if she had to go in his escape tunnel. He drew his feet up onto the toilet seat and hugged his knees tightly, burying his chin between them. Beth would *definitely* come: she was good at everything and always helped him if he was upset or worried … and he had never been as sad and scared in his life as he was now.

He put the spoon back in his pocket and let his legs dangle. He closed his eyes, pressed his palms against the sides of the cubicle and felt the equal and opposite force pushing back. The walls felt so solid it was (almost) like having two people stand guard beside him.

Yes - Beth would definitely come.

Chapter Eight
Convincing

Beth sat on her bed, picking at a loose thread on the hem of her T-shirt. Three weeks had passed since her encounter in the back of the van.

Her phone beeped, and another text came through from Melissa:

You'll have to talk about it eventually

Beth pressed 'delete'.
The phone beeped again.

Cowardy custard

It had been easy to avoid discussing the subject at school. It wasn't safe to speak anymore, even if she'd wanted to - the Headteacher had recruited a team of 'Super Prefects' to snitch on anti-Malvanian behaviour and now you couldn't trust anyone. And Melissa's relentless texts could be zapped into oblivion with the touch of a button. But Beth knew that even Melissa, lazy as she was, would eventually get bored with texting and try something else.

There was a cracking sound as something struck the bedroom window. Beth turned just in time to see a second stone strike the glass. She had been right: Melissa had finally dragged herself out of her bedroom and got on the bus. Beth tugged crossly at the loose thread and waited for her to go away.

Another text arrived.

I know you're in there you grumpy moo

Grudgingly, she fired a text back.

Could you try to be a bit more annoying?

She walked downstairs and opened the front door.

'Ha! Are your mum and dad in?' said Melissa.

Beth considered fibbing and saying her parents were at home, but Melissa could always spot a liar.

'Thought not!' Melissa breezed into the living room. 'Good. I can pinch some of your dad's chocolate …' She opened the sideboard and lifted the lid of a large box, quickly stuffing a chocolate in her mouth and throwing another one across the room for Beth to catch. Then she established herself on the sofa, draping her long arms over the tops of the cushions.

'And now we can talk.'

Beth looked at Melissa with reluctant admiration: tall and slender, afro hair, her caramel skin punctuated with freckles – and with more confidence than anyone she knew.

'I've been thinking,' said Melissa.

Unlikely, thought Beth.

'You want your brother back, right?'

Beth's heart heaved with pain. She nodded.

'Then you should go and get him.'

It was always that simple with Melissa.

'My dad says you should follow your dreams and not let people put you off.'

Beth watched her friend's dark eyes sparkle with self-belief. Melissa had such a tragic start in life: her mum died giving birth to her – but, as a consequence, she was more precious to her dad than most people could imagine. He had brought her up constantly telling her that she was special and beautiful and could have anything she wanted if she went looking for it. She loved herself, loved life and feared nothing. Beth often wished she could be more like her.

'But what about Mum and Dad?' said Beth. 'What if the Malvanians …?'

'I bet that driver guy was making it up. The syringe was probably full of lemonade.'

'But what if it wasn't?'

'Your parents want Peter back too, don't they? They'll be cool about it! They'll support you, no matter what you decide. That's what Dad says to me.'

Beth wasn't sure. She was still having nightmares about being driven round in the van.

'Look,' said Melissa. 'I didn't want to say this, but if the drugs thing is true …' She drummed her bright blue painted nails on a cushion. 'Then they might be doing bad stuff to Peter right now, and you need to save him.' She stopped the drumming to examine her nails at close quarters. 'Your mum and dad will be glad you did it. Dad says he would rather die than see me in pain. I bet your parents feel the same about Peter.'

It was difficult to argue with that.

'So, shall we make plans?' said Melissa.

Beth could feel her energy levels rising; Melissa was like some sort of life-force re-fuelling station.

She heard a key turn in the front door and then her parents entered the room, their faces glowing from a long walk.

'Hi there, Mr H!'

Her dad eyed Melissa with his usual look of affection and suspicion.

'Hello. Have you been stealing my chocolates again?'

'Yup,' beamed Melissa. 'How are you, Jane?'

'A bit hot, actually. Who'd like a nice cold drink?'

Beth watched her parents disappear into the kitchen, her mum apologising for the lack of choice when it came to fruit juice, and her dad talking about getting a padlock for the sideboard.

'See?' said Melissa. 'They'll be cool.'

***

'Room service!'

Beth had been spending a lot of time in her bedroom since the start of the school holidays. Her dad came in carrying a snack on a plate. She snapped shut a book called *'Eat Roots and Leaves! – Survival in the British Countryside'* and unsuccessfully tried to hide it under the bed.

'There's no need to be embarrassed,' said her dad.

'Some of the nicest donkeys I know eat stinging nettles.'

'Ha ha,' said Beth.

He put the plate down on the duvet and nodded towards the book. 'Homework, I presume.'

Beth nodded, but she couldn't look him in the eye.

'There's a soldier in the park,' her dad continued, 'stopping the kids from playing British Bulldog.'

'What does he want them to play instead? Malvanian Mongrels?'

'How about Malvanian Morons?'

'Or Mingers,' said Beth.

'I quite like Monkeybottoms myself.' He took a piece of apple from the plate. 'Did I tell you that when I see soldiers I imagine them wearing fairy costumes?' He chewed enthusiastically. 'A soldier doesn't look so clever in a pink dress. He thinks I'm scared of him; I think he's a big hairy girl. So I win. Little victories, you see. They're absolutely delicious.'

He helped himself to another apple slice, winked at her and left the room.

A text came in from Melissa.

All OK this end Have U tried pocket money trick? Trust me it works

Beth gathered her thoughts for a while then followed her dad downstairs.

'Didn't the butler bring enough food?' he said when he saw her.

Her mum was cleaning the grouting between the kitchen tiles with an old toothbrush and her dad was massaging her shoulders as she worked. Beth slipped between them, linked her arms with theirs and squeezed tightly.

'Hello – what's this?'

She made her eyes look as big and pathetic as possible.

'Can I have next month's pocket money early? I want to buy a new jacket.'

'Is that all darling?' said her mum. 'Of course you can.'

'I was going to say no,' said her dad.

Beth poked him in the ribs.

'No you weren't! And can I go to Melissa's for a sleepover tonight? I haven't seen her for a week.'

'Absolutely not, you're grounded!' He picked her up and dangled her upside down. Beth squealed in mock protest.

'Your wallet or mine, Janey?' said her dad.

'Seeing as you've got your hands full it had better be mine.' Her mum dried her hands and went in search of her handbag.

After being persuaded to help with the household chores in return for her pocket money advance, Beth returned to her room. She sat on her bedroom floor and put the bank notes in her purse with the other money she had saved. She had no idea if there was enough, but it was all she could get hold of. Melissa wouldn't have any to lend her; that much was certain. She pulled her rucksack from under the bed, pushed the purse inside and fastened the flap. She texted Melissa to say she would be round in three hours' time and headed to the bathroom for a shower.

The photo Beth had stolen from the album was one of her favourites. They were visiting a castle and her dad had balanced the camera on a section of ancient wall and set the self-timer. He had run round and sat down just in time. Her mum was looking at him and smiling; he was beaming at the camera as if to say 'Ha! I made it!'

Beth touched the photo gently. She and Peter were sitting in front of mum and dad, giving each other a bear hug, cheek to cheek.

Until today she hadn't noticed just how alike she and Peter were. Like peas in a pod. She put the photo inside a plastic bag to keep it dry, and slid it into a pocket inside the rucksack.

The rucksack felt heavy. Before she strapped it to her back she walked into Peter's room and sat on the bed. She picked up Jackson and stroked his ears.

'Guess what? You're coming with me, you scruffy old fluffbag.'

She pressed the teddy into the front pocket of the rucksack and zipped it up.

She walked downstairs and into the living room to say goodbye to her parents. As she stood in the doorway, her body framed by the woodwork, a look of horror spread over their faces.

'I'm only going to Melissa's,' she said. 'It's not Beaver sleepover – I'm coming back.'

But she knew it was a lie and she felt a wave of disgust leaching through her body.

They loved her. She could see it oozing out of them and

settling round them like an aura. She hugged them both, and it was the most painful thing she had ever done.

She kissed them, savouring the physical contact, skin against skin. She summoned up a smile from somewhere.

'See you Thursday,' she fibbed.

***

There was a Malvanian soldier sitting near the back of the bus.

'And where are you going, young lady?' he said.

His gun gave her the creeps, so she imagined him wearing a tutu and a pair of purple deely-boppers and suddenly he seemed completely harmless.

'A sleepover at my friend's house. In Prospect Street.'

'Sleepover. Dat is children's party, yes? You stay awake and tell ze silly stories, and keep ze parents awake too, yes? Dat is sleepover, I think'.

'Yes, that's sleepover,' said Beth, swapping the deely-boppers for a pink tiara and enjoying the fact that the soldier had no idea what she was thinking about. He nodded and smiled and turned to look out of the window.

Little victories, thought Beth. Dad was right – they *are* delicious.

Chapter Nine
Setting Out

Beth and Melissa huddled together in Melissa's kitchen in virtual darkness. The only light was coming from the clock on the cooker, which said *01:19* in a cold blue glow.

'Go girl - you can do it!' whispered Melissa.

A sound came from upstairs and the two froze, waiting for Melissa's dad to call out and ask them what they were doing. But nobody stirred, and the numbers on the clock changed silently to *01:20*.

'Just the house creaking,' said Melissa.

Beth expelled a faltering stream of air out of her mouth. 'Wish me luck!'

She opened the back door and breathed in the night air. Melissa kissed her on the cheek, closed the kitchen door and locked it. Through the glass, Beth watched Melissa wave and turn away, the tears on her cheeks twinkling blue as the oven clock said *01:21*.

She moved down the garden. Her heart was hammering so loudly against her ribs that she was sure the soldiers could hear it from the road. She peered over the garden gate and up the alleyway that ran between the back gardens and the street. She heard a cough, and a booted shadow with a gun passed from right to left across the alleyway entrance. She lifted her watch to her ear and counted the seconds. Exactly two and a half minutes later, the soldier went past again in the opposite direction.

It had been surprisingly easy to memorise the soldiers' movements. She knew that, when a soldier passed from right to left, she needed to count to sixty-five. Then the street would be empty for fifteen seconds. This would give her enough time to run up the alleyway, cross the road and disappear into the old footpath which was opposite Melissa's house. After fifteen seconds, the first of the soldiers would reappear around the corner and start to walk back along the street. Beth calculated that she would have eighteen seconds to get to the end of the path. By the time the soldier arrived at the footpath entrance, she would have climbed over the stile at the far end and made her escape into the countryside.

A boot scuffed on the pavement; a soldier appeared at the end of the alleyway and disappeared again like a ghost. Beth opened the gate and started counting. Adrenaline surged through her, daring her to count faster and faster, but she held her nerve and counted steadily to sixty-five. She skimmed up the alleyway, briefly stopping at the entrance to peer out into the street. Just as she had predicted, neither of the soldiers was in sight. She slipped into the road and ran across it. Compared to the darkness of the alleyway the street lamps were bright and exposing, compelling her to keep moving. This is so easy, she thought. Stupid Malvanians; anyone could do this. She forged ahead, past the post box and in front of the house that stood next to the old footpath. Then she dodged into the footpath entrance.

Immediately she could see that the stile at the far end was blocked. She jolted to a halt, her trainers squeaking on the tarmac. Of course the Malvanians had closed such an obvious escape route. Now who was stupid? The stile was barricaded with wooden boards to a height of two metres, and loops of razor wire were coiled over it, their deadly thorns glinting under the footpath lights. She searched for an alternative escape route. But there was no choice: she must run towards the wooden wall with its crown of spikes. She heard a soldier clear his throat. He could only be twenty metres away from her, and the distance to the barricade was twice that far. She gritted her teeth and forced herself to run faster than she'd ever run before.

She sprang forwards, her arms punching the air, propelling herself towards the end of the footpath. At the very last second – the barricade just a metre in front of her – she dived into a hedge. It took forever to reach the ground, and fragments of twig bounced down through the branches around her, sounding far too loud in the tranquillity of the night. She lay still, sharp sticks digging into her neck and jabbing her in the kidneys. From the end of the footpath a tense and penetrating voice rang out.

'Who goes there? Show yourself!'

Beth didn't move. The soldier called out in Malvanian to his partner, and shouted again.

'Show yourself immediately!'

There was a long pause. The two soldiers conversed in low voices. Then, in the still night air, she heard them both cock their weapons.

'You must show yourself!' came the cry, and two pairs of steel-capped boots began to walk up the path. They came nearer and nearer, and Beth closed her eyes, refusing to believe that she had failed before her journey had even begun.

Chapter Ten
Struggle

There was a terrible yowl and a rustling in the bushes, and one of the soldiers shouted.

'*Haltzen! Haltzen!* Stay where you are!'

There was more rustling, and a strange, strangled screech. The other soldier started laughing.

'*Dat is Katzer!* You want to shoot the little *Katzer?* Go ahead, you big, brave man!'

The first soldier cursed in Malvanian, and the two men retreated down the path. Beth waited until the soldiers' voices had faded out of earshot. She crawled through the bushes on her hands and knees until she had bypassed the barricade and reached the fence that bordered the field. She squeezed through, then stopped and sat on the grass.

Gradually her breathing returned to normal and her drilling heartbeat subsided to a gentle thump. She rested her chin on her knees and wondered how many soldiers were patrolling the countryside; the rumour was that it was not many. A breeze wafted a parcel of noise towards her, magnifying the sound of the Malvanian soldiers chatting at the *Kantonlein* checkpoint, about a hundred metres to the east. A motorbike revved up, and she heard the electronic beeping signal of the barrier being raised. The motorbike engine roared, then disappeared to a distant purr as the bike sped along the road that led out of town. The barrier siren beeped again.

She stood up, her jeans damp from sitting on the grass. As she inched forward, getting used to the feel of the ground underfoot, a puff of pungent cigarette smoke and a ripple of laughter floated towards her from the Malvanians at the barrier. The crescent moon provided only a dim sliver of light and it was difficult to see where she was going. But she knew these fields well, and was confident that she could find her way across them and arrive safely at the charcoal burners' hut. It was four and a half miles away.

As she walked she imagined a group of Malvanian soldiers occupying the hut, guns poking from every window and cigarette butts littering the clearing - and prayed it would be empty. She reached out and touched the fence at the side of the field, and felt her way along it until she came to its corner. She turned left, continuing to use the fence to guide her. There was a steady upward slope, and the weight of the rucksack on her back and the sticky grass around her ankles made it feel much steeper than usual. The ground was uneven, and in the dark she was unable to see the tussocks under her feet, which caused her to stumble as she walked. Within minutes her thighs were aching. It took much longer than she expected to reach the fence on the far side of the field, and when she got to the stile she sat on the step. She reached into her pocket and pulled out a half-eaten *Lipschmacke* chocolate bar, broke off two squares and put them in her mouth. She set off again, and for a short while the chocolate acted as an anaesthetic, soothing her aching legs.

Her head started to throb and she stopped to take some painkillers. She unscrewed the cap of a large bottle of mineral water and raised the tablets to her mouth. She was surprised to discover that her hands were shaking and as she attempted to push the pills between her lips they fell to the ground. She knelt down, wedging the bottle in the mud, but the tablets were lost in the dirt. She reached for the rucksack to dispense a fresh dose and knocked the water bottle over with her elbow. Half of its contents leaked away into the earth and her head thumped even harder.

The next field had been planted with wheat, and Beth could smell the unripe grains as the stems brushed against her left hip. The soft, ploughed soil sucked her feet downwards and the pain in her thighs spread upwards into her lower back. Her sense of balance was impaired in the dark, and when her foot struck a large piece of flint she toppled over, twisting her ankle. The ligaments wrenched apart as she fell and landed on her back. She yelled, drawing her knee up to her chest and cupping her hands around the injury that already felt as if someone had stuck a red-hot knife in it.

She rocked herself backwards and forwards until the pain became less acute. She had a bandage in her first aid kit, and she knew she should bind her leg as soon as possible, but the spongy soil felt comfy and soothing beneath her, and induced a strong desire to sleep. She tried to sit herself up, battling against the weighty pull of her rucksack, but it was too much effort and she sank back again. Her ankle now pulsated hypnotically, and, gazing at the stars, her eyes fluttered closed.

When she woke the air was cooler, and the ears of wheat were shushing gently in the breeze. She shone her torch at her watch: she had been asleep for over an hour, and it would be difficult to get to the hut before dawn broke.

She hurriedly brushed the dirt from her clothes and pushed on. Defying her weary muscles and throbbing ankle, she dug her trainers into the soft, lumpy earth and worked her calves to keep moving forward. Four fields later she limped to the top of the hill and, leaning forward and gripping the fence with both hands, stopped to catch her breath. About three miles below her in the dark was the copse and the charcoal burners' hut.

Ages later she climbed over the final stile. Her legs were screaming with exhaustion and her trainers were chewing up her feet. In front of her was a half-mile stretch of uncultivated land - and the copse lay on the other side of it. She trudged onwards and eventually became aware that there were low clumps of vegetation sprouting out of the ground and she knew she was almost there.

A loud clatter of voices suddenly came out of the dark, and the field seemed to come alive. Something smacked her in the chest then scratched her across the cheek. Caught off balance, she tumbled to the ground. Her face buried in the mud, there was a scuffle immediately to her right, and the hair on the back of her head rippled as something large brushed against her.

Chapter Eleven
Alone

Beth lifted her face from the soil and spat out a tuft of grass. A rapid peeping noise erupted from the ground right in front of her, and the smell of feathers and bird droppings penetrated her nostrils. A gaggle of baby pheasants was crying out in distress a few centimetres from her face.

She pulled herself to her feet, stepped round the nest and continued towards the copse. She could hear the adult birds circling above, and flinched every time they called out, desperately hoping that she wouldn't disturb any more of their young. Being smacked in the face by an angry pheasant was not something she wanted to experience again.

She picked her way through the trees. Her heart leapt with joy when she saw the hut, now the faintest of silhouettes against a slightly lighter sky. There were no lights and no voices. She walked more quickly, happy memories coming back to her - Melissa sitting on the rickety old table and stuffing a whole packetful of crisps into her mouth at once; spilling fizzy drink on the floor and then screaming for hours when thousands of ants streamed into the hut to hoover up the sugar; watching, motionless, as a robin sang from a branch near the window, then feeding it by hand with a currant bun.

She went inside. In the half-light the hut looked grim. It stank of neglect and decay. She allowed her body to sink into one of the chairs, but it was damp and smelled revolting, and a film of filth came off on her hands. She shone her torch around the hut, and the feeble beam of light exaggerated the dark corners and cast creepy shadows onto the walls.

Pinned to the backroom door was a faded list in Melissa's handwriting: '*Things We Can Do Without Annoying Parents Hanging Around To Tell Us Off*'. The fetid dampness rose from the chair, through her clothes and into her skin, and a chill spiralled through her. She opened her rucksack and sought comfort in a cereal bar but the dank odour of the hut tainted it as she ate.

What had she done? The chewed-up oats and raisins clagged in her throat. It wasn't supposed to be like this. She was stuck in a foul place, a ghastly halfway house, with her parents too far away to look after her - and with Peter way, way out of reach.

She rolled out her sleeping bag and, fully clothed, climbed inside until her head was covered. The unyielding floor greeted her bones unfeelingly and she could hear things scuttling about just centimetres from her face. She clasped Jackson under her chin and, as the light from the morning sun diffused across the sky above her, she descended into a series of disturbed dreams about poisoned chocolate, pheasant soldiers with guns - and her parents weeping and calling for her across the fields.

***

The sun was bright and high in the sky when Jane Hardy finished cleaning the kitchen. As she wrung out the dishcloth and folded it, she caught sight of her reflection in the gleaming kettle. Golly, I've lost weight, she thought. She checked the kitchen clock: it was nearly eleven. She looked around for a new task to keep herself occupied, and noticed that Beth had left one of her hair scrunchies in the fruit bowl. She picked it up, stretched it between her fingers and breathed in deeply. It smelt of Beth. She got a duster out of the cupboard and made her way upstairs, humming to herself and taking the steps two at a time. As she passed Peter's bedroom, she paused and blew a kiss through the doorway, then she turned the handle on Beth's door and entered.

The room wasn't particularly messy: there was a half-empty mug of coffee on the desk, Beth's dressing gown was on the floor, there were a couple of bits of paper lying around, and body glitter was scattered on the carpet. She put the scrunchie back in Beth's hair accessory box and hung up the dressing gown. She scooped up the two pieces of paper, and was about to throw them in the bin when she noticed that one of them had '*To Mum and Dad*' written on the front. She raised her eyebrows. Beth usually wrote them a note if she had a confession to make – like the time she and Melissa accidentally spilt nail varnish on a cushion and tried to wipe it off with toilet cleaner.

'What have you done now, darling?' she said, glancing across at the body glitter on the floor. 'Nothing looks too bad.'

She opened the note. Before she could read three

sentences, she lurched across the bedroom and was violently sick in the waste paper basket.

***

Beth was woken by a wood pigeon cooing from the rafters of the charcoal burners' refuge. She could tell by the strength of the light coming in through the roof that it was nearly midday. The misery of being alone was matched by a searing pain in her ankle, and she rolled up her trouser leg to inspect the damage. The flesh had swollen to twice its normal size and was ballooning out of the top of her trainer like a soufflé. She found her first aid kit and bound it up to limit the swelling, then hobbled into the small clearing at the front of the hut, sat on the grass and let the sunshine soak into her skin.

Feeling a little brighter, she took her phone out of her pocket and flicked it open. Just one call would be ok, wouldn't it? She accessed the Phonebook and, as she lifted her hand to shield the display from the sun, her sleeve slipped down to reveal the scars where the Malvanian driver had handcuffed her to the inside of the *Komplianz* van.

'Everyone in my family will be punished because I have been a naughty girl…'

She snapped the phone shut. Despite the noonday sun she felt freezing again.

She limped to the edge of the copse to scan the fields and was relieved to see they were completely free of Malvanian troops. She gathered up some dry sticks, took them to the old brazier and, using dead leaves for kindling, she lit a fire. Then she went to the water butt at the back of the hut for a wash. The water had bits of debris floating in it that clung to her skin and scratched her. When she washed her face, a crusty smear of dried blood appeared on her flannel, so she searched in her wash bag for a mirror. An angry-looking scratch cast a vivid line of scarlet across her cheek where the pheasant had snagged her the night before. She dabbed some antiseptic cream into the wound, and it began to emit tiny pulses of pain. Biting her lip, she brushed her hair carefully and scraped it back into a scrunchie. Then she took out her *Candy Phlox* lipstick and deftly applied it. She tilted her head defiantly to one side.

'That's better,' she said.

She filled the empty water bottle from the butt, wondering why on earth she had decided to wash in it first. Out in the clearing, she boiled the water and tried to heat up some noodles. But the fire became erratic and the pasta ended up lukewarm and barely cooked. She tried to take the taste away with a mug of tepid coffee with six sugars, but it remained disgusting.

***

August 8th

Dear Mum and Dad,

I'm <u>so</u> sorry. I've gone to get Peter back.
Please, please, please don't be cross with me. I saw him on tv and I know where he is. I promise I'll keep myself safe and we will BOTH be back soon. Don't tell anyone that I've gone.

Love you so much,
Beth. xxxxxxx

P.S. I lied about that jacket so I could get you to give me the pocket money. Sorry. xxx
P.P.S. Burn this or something after you've read it. x

Jane stood with Doug by the kitchen sink, watching Beth's letter shrivel up into a scrap of black ash. The taste of vomit still lingered in her mouth; her eyes felt as if they were half-closed, her eyelids gorged with fluid from hours of crying. She heard herself emit a low moan as Doug turned on the tap to extinguish the dying flames and wash the remains of the letter away.

'What are we going to do?' she murmured.

Doug buried his face in his hands and massaged his forehead with his fingers.

'You know what they did to Mary Fullager when she tried to escape.'

She stared dumbly at him. The name wouldn't compute.

'The head of maths at Beth's school. They caught up with her about a mile from the detention centre. Took her to the Korrection Unit and injected her with drugs until she stopped protesting. Then they took her twelve-year-old daughter to see her and told her she'd end up the same way unless she joined the Malvanian Youth. Then they paid Mary's brother a visit and beat up the whole family.'

She leant over the sink and retched again. Her abdomen ached from being sick so many times – yet the rest of her was so numb she was bored by the repetition of it.

'There's only one thing we can do, my love,' said Doug. He raised one hand to his forehead again and clutched at the skin. 'Absolutely nothing.'

She didn't want to hear it. She pushed herself upright, away from the sink and, buoyed by an adrenaline surge that had accompanied the vomiting, strode across the kitchen, picked up the telephone and scrolled down the menu to find Beth's mobile number. Doug darted across the kitchen and, cradling his hand around hers, ended the call before it had begun.

'They could be listening in – tracing the call! We can't, Jane!'

She sank to a crouching position on the floor. Doug joined her, clasped his arms around her and rocked her backwards and forwards. He buried his face in her neck and she could feel his tears soaking into her collar.

Her babies had gone and she wished she were dead.

Chapter Twelve
Trying

Doug released Jane from his arms and, with some urgency, stood up. It was important to keep busy and find solutions – and he was encouraged by a new idea.

'Aunty Mu!' he said.

He moved across the kitchen and began to rummage in the bits-and-bobs drawer.

'It's in here somewhere ...'

Jane did not move. She looked too tired to care.

'I knew it! Good old Mu.' He waved an outdated mobile phone. 'Don't you remember? We kept it when we cleared the house after the funeral. Beth didn't want it - but it's got fifteen quid of credit on it. And it's registered to Mu so if they trace the call they won't know it's coming from us. At least, I think that's how it works.' He rejoined Jane on the floor. 'Do you want to give it a go?'

Jane kissed her forefinger and planted it on Doug's lips. 'I thought they could track the position of the phone.'

'This is 'pay as you go'. That makes a difference, doesn't it? Wasn't there something on that police drama? All the criminals use 'pay as you go' so they can't be traced.'

'If you're sure ...' Jane took the phone. 'Actually I

think it only had three pounds credit left.'

Doug pulled a face.

'OK – one phone call and the rest in texts.'

Jane dialled the number. From the expression on her face he could see that it had gone straight to the answering machine.

'Bethy?' Her voice cracked. 'It's Mum.' She spoke the words in a whisper before drying up completely.

He looked at her in desperation, silently beseeching her to say *something* before too many precious seconds ticked by. He snatched the phone from her.

'Daddy's here, darling. We're worried about you. Text this number and let us know you're all right - and do it soon.' It was the turn of his voice to disintegrate. 'We love you, Squidgy.'

He terminated the call, and the house seemed to ache with emptiness.

At the end of the garden, the gate clicked open and clunked shut, and a familiar voice called out.

'Anybody home?'

'It's Stone,' said Doug.

'I can't face him,' said Jane. She walked into the hallway and went upstairs.

Mr Stone's pointy face leered round the kitchen door.

'Mind if I come in?' he said, already halfway through the doorway.

'Suit yourself,' said Doug.

'I will,' said Stone. His eyes narrowed behind his glasses and he scrutinised Doug's tired face.

'Are you all right?' he asked.

'Oh, rotten day at work, you know. Spent the whole

day squinting at spreadsheets - it makes your eyes water.'

Mr Stone nodded. He screwed up his nose and sniffed round the room. 'Can I smell burning?'

'I just knocked the roll of kitchen towel onto the gas ring. It made quite a stink.'

'Yes, it would, it would … Is young Beth here? I have something to give her.'

Doug told him that Beth was staying at Melissa's for a couple of days.

'She's a good girl, that one. Very … sensible.' said Mr Stone. He held up a Malvanian Youth activity leaflet. 'I'll leave this here for her, if I may. I won't take up any more of your time – Phyllis will be dishing up tea in a minute.'

He turned to go, then hesitated and called up the stairs.

'No need to hide from me next time, Mrs H! I don't bite, you know!'

Doug watched Mr Stone leave the garden. He picked up the Malvanian Youth pamphlet, threw it into the sink and lit another match. As the flames licked around the paper, he heard Jane come downstairs. He saw her walk past the kitchen, eyes glazed over and not seeing him. She switched on the television and, as the small fire in the sink flared up and devoured the last of the leaflet, Doug stepped into the living room and watched her stare blankly at the TV screen, completely in a world of her own.

Chapter Thirteen
Control

Phyllis Stone pottered into the room to find her husband hunched over his computer keyboard. The light from the monitor was shining on his forehead, and he breathed heavily as he tapped the computer keys with his bony forefingers. His face twitched as she approached him, and he clicked on the mouse.

'Coffee and macaroons,' she said. 'I'm not late, am I dear?'

It was exactly five to eleven.

'No, no, my dear. Ever punctual. You're a good old girl.'

She placed a wooden tray on the desk, and a bone china cup wobbled in its saucer.

'Don't spill it, woman!' said Harold. 'You'll blow up the computer!'

The oven pinger went off downstairs, and he fired an expectant look at her.

'I'd better see to those hard boiled eggs,' she said, and obediently went downstairs.

She stared vacantly as a stream of water gushed from the cold tap onto a saucepan of eggs in the sink. The radio was broadcasting an interview with the Malvanian Minister of Discipline.

'The Women's Institute in Swansea has been punished appropriately …' said the Minister.

'A quantity of nostalgic British photographs was seized from the meeting hall this afternoon …'

'The viewing of illegal material will not be tolerated…'

'I do not consider the use of truncheons excessive … these foolish women need to understand the seriousness of their crime … they will be sent to a *Korrection* Unit to be re-educated …'

Phyllis was hardly listening. She never understood what the government people were talking about; she only listened to the radio because it made a nice, friendly noise in the background. She turned off the tap, left the eggs to cool down and arranged a few more macaroons on a plate to take round to next door. She swapped her brown slippers for a pair of brown shoes and went out.

There was no reply from the Hardys, so she decided to take the macaroons over to Mr Jafary. She pressed the doorbell and giggled as it played a tune that was familiar to her. Mr Jafary appeared at the door and invited her in.

'How wonderful to see you, Phyllis,' said Mr Jafary, 'and I have the perfect accompaniment to those delicious-looking biscuits.' He led her into the kitchen, picked up a decorative black and gold tin and twisted off the lid with a flourish.

***

Mr Stone picked up three macaroons and poked them all into his mouth at once. The biscuits cracked between his teeth, and he retrieved the web page that he had minimised when his wife had entered the room: the homepage of the Malvanian People's Party. He resumed his predatory position over the keyboard, and jabbed a short phrase into the 'search' box. A new page appeared:

'ZEE GLÖBALIZERUND OB ZEE IDENTITEN
MALVANISCH'
'The Globalisation of Malvanian Identity.'

His teeth clacked on the last remnants of macaroon, and he began to read with interest.

***

'Finest Darjeeling tea!' said Mr Jafary. 'A most delicate taste that will be complimented perfectly by your superior home baking!'

Phyllis blushed. Harold never spoke to her like that.

She watched Mr Jafary warm the pot and arrange the macaroons on a plate. Tea was becoming a luxury. As part of the Malvanian Government's 'Improvements', only coffee was being imported into the country. Mr Jafary guided her to the comfy chair by the window and poured the tea, taking care to give her exactly the right amount of milk. During a lull in the conversation, she idly watched a Malvanian soldier walk down the street. Mr Jafary eyed him too, and sprang from his armchair.

'Please, come and see my pride and joy – it would be such an honour if you did!'

She followed Mr Jafary into the dining room. It was full of royal family memorabilia. Every surface was a sumptuous display of gold, red, white and blue. There were cups, plates, vases, tankards and porcelain sweet jars, all bearing portraits to commemorate royal events. There were embellished biscuit tins and quaint-looking tin trays, dolls of royal family members, gaudy key rings and other trinkets. Displayed above the sideboard was a large Union Jack tea towel, and taking pride of place over the mantelpiece was an elegant framed photograph of the Queen. Phyllis chuckled and said it was a very pretty collection.

'It was the worst day of my life when they put the royal family in prison,' said Mr Jafary.

Phyllis nodded politely. She thought it was a shame that the Queen had been taken away, but she wasn't keen on some of the others, like Anne or Charles. She was surprised to see Mr Jafary had a Union Jack, because she knew it was illegal to own one, but she couldn't really see the harm in a silly old tea towel.

'Every night, my dear, I pray to God that Her Majesty is safe and sound,' said Mr Jafary. 'She is a wonderful woman, and I truly believe that one day she will return and save us all.'

Phyllis had nothing new to say, and repeated that it was a very pretty little collection indeed. Then she glanced at the royal wedding ornamental clock and saw that it was a quarter to one. She must get back home and prepare lunch. She thanked Mr Jafary for his hospitality, and he gave her back the plate and shook her hand.

'Do come again, my dear,' he said.

When she crossed the road, the jolly tune from Mr Jafary's doorbell popped into her head again. As she let herself in through the front door, she started humming it to herself. She changed back into her slippers and went upstairs to get Harold's elevenses tray. As she approached the spare room she burst into song.

'Land of hope and glory, mother of the free …'

She opened the door – and then she stopped singing. A feeling of terror crept over her.

Harold was staring at her with a vile and hateful look. The colour had drained from his skin so that his lips were as white as a piece of veal, and his eyes were flashing with a fury that she had learnt to dread.

'How dare you sing that filth in this house,' he rasped.

'I … I didn't realise what it was, Harold – I swear to God! I just took the macaroons to Mr Jafary, and the little tune was playing on his doorbell, and I started singing it completely by accident, you know, how tunes get into your head sometimes! I just wasn't thinking, I …'

'You stupid little bitch,' he said.

'Please, don't hurt me.'

And then she realised that she had a way out. If Harold had someone else to hate, then he wouldn't harm her.

'And that's not all he has in his house!' she blabbed. 'He has a whole room full of patriotic trinkets – and very pretty they are too!' (She told herself that if she complimented Mr Jafary it would somehow lessen the betrayal.) 'And there is a big picture of the Queen and a Union Jack as well! And he said that he prays for the Queen to save us from the evil Malvanians every night! There's even a music box that plays 'God Save the Queen'!'

She stopped. She could tell by the look on Harold's face that she had said enough. The colour was returning to his cheeks and the threat of violence was leaking out of the room like water going down a plug hole. Harold nodded and waved her out of the room with a cursory gesture. She moved towards him to pick up the tray.

'Leave it!' he snapped, and she scuttled out of the room.

***

Harold navigated his way around the Malvanian People's Party website. He found a link called:

'*NOCHTS GEFOLLGEN.*
Non-Cooperation'.

Then he found a sub-heading entitled:

'*REPÖRTZ!*
– Reporting Offenders'.

In the top right hand corner of the screen was an icon that said:

'*KONTAKT*'

He activated the mouse a final time, flexed his fingers and began to type.

Chapter Fourteen
Assault

Doug woke at 3am. The other half of the bed was cold. The bedroom door was ajar, allowing a dim glow of light to leak into the bedroom, and the sound of rattling crockery was coming from the kitchen. He pulled himself out of bed, fumbled for his dressing gown and went downstairs. Jane was doing the washing up in her nightie.

'Join me in a cup of coffee, love?'

As he unscrewed the coffee jar and spooned some granules into a mug, he caught sight of his reflection in the darkened window. There was no mistaking the dark rings round his eyes and his gaunt cheekbones. We both look so old, he thought as he looked at Jane's tiny, shell-shocked body stooping over the sink.

A muffled sound came through the wall. The Stones' kitchen adjoined the Hardys'.

'I tell you, he's spying on us,' he whispered.

'No - it'll just be Phyllis,' breathed Jane. 'Her stomach ulcer's playing up again, she said.'

He walked to the kitchen table and wrote something on a piece of paper. He held it up so Jane could see it:

Why are we speaking really quietly, then?

Jane smiled and playfully threw a tea towel at him.

'Look at us – we're in a silly old state, aren't we?'

'I think we're doing pretty ruddy well, given the circumstances,' he said.

There was another noise, this time from the street, and he went to the front room to investigate.

A Malvanian army vehicle had parked on the opposite side of the road, and there was a pack of Malvanian soldiers skulking in Mr Jafary's front garden. On command, they pounced on the front door. They kicked it until it gave way, then surged inside shouting: 'Surrender yourself! Surrender!'

Jane also came to the window and, after fifteen minutes, the soldiers reappeared, walked to their lorry in single file and embarked. The lorry sped away into the night, leaving Mr Jafary's front door hanging in its frame like a loose tooth dangling from a thread of skin.

Taking Jane by the hand, Doug went outside and hurried across the street.

He groped his way along Mr Jafary's darkened hallway, stumbling over broken bits of wood.

'Mohinder?' he called. There was no reply.

Jane had edged into the dining room and turned on the light. Doug heard her gasp and followed her inside. Glass crunched beneath his slippers. The dining room table had been uprooted and turned on its side. The chairs were smashed and the carpet was littered with broken china and glass. The portrait of the Queen had been ripped apart and Mr Jafary's collection of royal family dolls had been dismembered and the heads and limbs gruesomely discarded. A piece of cloth lay in front of the upturned sideboard. Doug picked it up and saw that it was half a Union Jack that had been ripped from end to end. He walked back into the hall and up the stairs. The bathroom light was on and the door partly open.

Mr Jafary was crumpled on the floor between the toilet and the wall, and he had been blindfolded using the other half of the Union Jack. Doug untied it, and Mr Jafary winced in the bright light. His pyjamas were streaked with blood, and a congealing blood clot was hanging from his nose. His hair was soaked from having his head thrust down the toilet.

'My God, Mohinder, what have they done to you?'

Mr Jafary lifted his pyjama top to reveal a body covered in bruises. Jane arrived at the top of the stairs and her hand shot towards her mouth in horror.

'Could I ask you, my dear, to put the kettle on,' said Mr Jafary, 'a cup of Darjeeling and I'll be right as rain in no time.'

***

Jane went back down the stairs and into the kitchen. She touched the kitchen light switch and the neon bulb flickered into life. The contents of Mr Jafary's kitchen bin were scattered over the floor and sprinkled over the top of it were the precious contents of the little black and gold tea caddy.

***

Beth woke at about five in the morning with a sense that she was not alone. She heard a twig snap close behind her, and twisted around in her sleeping bag. Standing a couple of metres from her head was a fox, its dark eyes assessing the danger. Its auburn fur glowed in the early light – and then, suddenly spooked, it darted away and took cover under a bank of blackberry bushes.

She sat up and rubbed her face. Every muscle in her body was hurting. She dragged herself out of the sleeping bag, and as she stood up her stomach let out a hungry moan. She walked over to the bank of brambles in search of breakfast. The blackberries were plump and ripe, and came away from their stalks so easily that it was as if the bush was giving the berries to her. They tasted sweet and fresh, and the sugar rush they gave her made her eat faster and faster, gorging on as many berries as she could at a time, the juice running down her chin and colouring her fingers dark purple. The sun caressed the back of her neck and warmed her aching body, and she began to believe that she had the strength to continue on her journey.

She took her mobile phone out of her pocket, switched it on and listened to her parents' message for the seventh time. A new text had come in from them:

Stay safe darling – Love you.

Definitely from Mum, that one. Dad had taken to sending military-style messages:

Chin up Squidgy – Roger and Out

She keyed in her reply:

Doing OK Bit tired Love U

Another twig snapped behind her. Then came a swish in the grass. A hand clamped itself onto her mouth, jerking her body backwards. She whimpered and dropped the phone. Her stomach knotted tightly and the blackberries curdled inside her. Someone pressed a cold barrel of metal to her throat and cocked the trigger.

'Don't make a sound and don't try to escape,' he said. Then he put a hood over her head, tied her hands behind her back, and picked her up and carried her away.

Chapter Fifteen
Capture

Beth's body jerked with every step her abductor took. Her head collided with his back every time his feet struck the ground. Beneath the darkness of the hood she felt sick, and as more and more blood rushed to her head she began to see stars. She stifled a moan, fearing she would be shot if she made a noise.

The running stopped. A door opened and she was carried through the corridors of some sort of building. Now she could hear a second set of footsteps behind her. The person carrying her paused, and another door clicked open. She was swiftly turned the right way up and placed on a chair; she swooned as the blood drained out of her head. The hood was pulled off and she found herself looking across a table at a tall, muscular man wearing camouflage gear.

'Are you all right?' he said sternly. His accent was English. She nodded.

In the doorway stood a man with a beard. He was holding her rucksack. He took out her mobile phone and the first man glared at her.

'We've been watching you,' he said. 'Do you realise you had that on long enough for the Malvanians to get a trace on your position?' He turned to the bearded man. 'Dispose of it immediately. And get her a glass of water.'

The bearded man nodded and left.

'And as for the bloody stupid fire you lit...' He frowned. 'What were you doing out there? Start by telling me your name and where you come from.'

He let her talk, never taking his eyes off her, watching every flicker on her face and analysing the inflections in her voice. When she had finished, he nodded.

'I see you have the best of intentions, but you will never get into London. The Malvanian forces have tanks and helicopters, night vision cameras and soldiers who have been instructed to kill on sight. It would be impossible.'

The door opened and the bearded man returned. He signalled to his colleague and handed him a leaflet, saying something in a low voice. The tall man threw the paper into Beth's lap. It was her application form for the Malvanian Youth.

'How do you explain that?' he said.

He calmly reached inside his jacket and pulled out a gun. 'Perhaps you are not as loyal to this country as you should be.'

He placed the gun on the table in front of him. His fingertips twitched towards the trigger.

'Well?'

Beth tried to speak but her mouth was so dry that her tongue had stuck to the roof of her mouth. The man edged his fingers forwards until they were touching the grip of the gun handle.

'Please don't hurt me...' She prised her tongue off her teeth and spoke in a faint croak. 'I didn't know about the helicopters and the night cameras!'

The man's hand curled round the gun and he lifted it slowly.

'I was going to join the Malvanian Youth so I could be with Peter!' She started to cry. 'I hate the Malvanians!'

She forced the rest of her words out between sobs, telling the man about Mr Stone giving her the application form.

'Ian, stop.'

The bearded man stepped forward. 'She can only be thirteen. I think we can say that she isn't a threat.'

The man withdrew the gun. The bearded man untied her hands and gave her a glass of water. She tried to drink, but she was shaking too much and the glass rattled against her teeth.

'I'm Roger Clough,' said the second man, 'and this is Ian Forsyth. He's in charge here.'

'Hello,' said Forsyth. He reached out and shook her hand. 'I'm sorry about the interrogation, but it was necessary. It's vital we know who's on our side.'

Beth nodded. 'Who are you?' she said.

'I'll explain in detail later,' said Forsyth. 'All you need to know for now is that we are members of the British Resistance. Now, if you'll excuse us, we have work to do. I'll arrange for someone to bring you food.'

The two men left the room.

She slumped back in her chair and stared at a greasy mark on the wall. Twenty-five minutes passed without her realising it, then a new face appeared at the doorway, carrying a tray of food.

'Hi, I'm Ricky. Ricky Forsyth. That was my dad giving you a hard time.'

Ricky was about seventeen. He had a tall, lean body and wavy blond hair. He grinned and his blue eyes sparkled.

'Grub's up,' he said.

Beth tucked in to a steaming plate of corned beef hash, mashed potato and turnips. She would have turned her nose up at it if she'd been offered it at home, but today it tasted like heaven. Ricky watched her eat, his eyes shining.

'Hungry girl,' he said.

There was a bowl of crumble and custard for pudding and a cup of tea made with condensed milk. She flopped backwards and looked at Ricky's face. He was very good looking, and the khaki coloured military clothes that he was wearing made him look exciting. She could see his chest muscles under his T-shirt.

'Are you the army, then?' she said.

'No. The British Resistance is mainly civilians. Everyday folk like me and my dad. The people in charge are mostly army personnel though.'

'Are they here too?'

'No - there are just twenty of us here. We're called a cell. There are secret cells all over the country, some hiding in bunkers like this one – and others working under cover in towns and cities - all waiting to rise up and chuck the Malvanians out of the country. And while we're waiting we keep fit and practice our skills. That's how we found you: Dad and Roger were on an 'invisibility' exercise. Which is why they saw you but you didn't see them.'

He jumped up.

'Come on, let me show you something.'

She followed him out of the room and along a series of

corridors, until they came to an office full of computers and communications equipment. A man was sitting with his back to them looking at the internet, and he swivelled round on his chair when he heard them come in.

'Wally, this is Beth the fugitive,' said Ricky.

'Good afternoon, Beth.'

She couldn't believe it: the man at the computer was Mr Dyche, the History teacher who was missing from school.

'Wally is searching for communications from our leader,' explained Ricky.

Dyche invited Beth to sit down next to him.

I can't believe he's called Wally, she thought; Melissa will scream with laughter when I tell her.

'Now then, intrepid young lady,' said Mr Dyche. 'You probably don't want to hear this, but I'm going to give you a History lesson.'

Beth rolled her eyes.

'You will have learnt a bit about the Second World War at primary school – about the evacuees and so forth, yes?'

She nodded.

'And you know that Winston Churchill was the Prime Minister?'

She didn't know but she nodded again.

'Well, he was a very clever man – unlike the fool who's in charge today. Churchill knew that the Germans might invade Britain, so he organised a secret army. They were called the British Resistance Movement. They were organised into small groups - each one so secret that nobody knew where the other groups were, or who was in them.'

'So, if one group was captured, they couldn't snitch on the others,' said Ricky.

Dyche continued. 'And, if the Germans had invaded, the Resistance would have hidden away and waited to be told what to do. And that's what we're doing now.'

'Only we're bigger and better,' said Ricky. 'We've got computer technology so we can do stuff without being noticed. We've had our names wiped off every database so the Malvanians don't know we exist. Army records were faked so that nobody knew weapons were being moved around the country.'

Her head was spinning. There were so many questions she wanted to ask.

'But I can see you are tired,' said Mr Dyche.

He picked up a telephone and dialled. A woman's voice talked faintly at the other end.

'Our new recruit is ready for you now,' he said.

The woman soon appeared and introduced herself as Julie Lockwood.

'Time to show you your quarters,' she said.

'See you later, little miss fugitive,' said Ricky, touching Beth on the arm.

Julie led her to another part of the bunker and showed her where she could shower and sleep. After Julie left the room, Beth stroked her forearm where Ricky had touched her and her heart rippled inside her. Then she caught sight of herself in the mirror. Her eyes were red and swollen from crying and she had blackberry juice stains down her chin. Oh great, she thought, I meet the most gorgeous boy in the country and I look like a puffed-up pig with a purple beard. No wonder he kept smiling at me. She undressed, jumped into the shower and washed away every last bit of embarrassment.

Chapter Sixteen
Desperate Times, Desperate Measures

A loud bell rang in the corridor outside the dormitory. Julie appeared at the bathroom door, rubbing her hair dry with a towel.

'Time to get up, soldier,' she said. 'No lie-ins here, not even for unexpected guests.'

A khaki shirt and trousers and a pair of army boots had been laid out for her, and Beth washed and dressed quickly.

Another bell sounded.

'Breakfast time,' said Julie. 'I'll show you to the mess room.'

As they walked, Beth asked Julie how she joined the Resistance.

'I'm a journalist,' she said. 'I've written several articles criticising the government's defence cuts. Last year, I got a phone call from a man who said he had some information about the Malvanian army. I agreed to meet him at a busy café, and the man who turned up was Forsyth. He asked me what I thought about the rumours that Malvania was preparing to invade Britain. I said I believed the country was in terrible danger; that the Prime Minister was too concerned with his own image to notice that Malvania was a threat. I told him I wanted to write an article about the government putting popularity before freedom. Forsyth signed me up there and then.'

'What if you'd said no?' said Beth. 'You could have told everyone about the Resistance.'

'Forsyth's clever. He knew I'd say yes.'

Beth nodded, impressed by Forsyth's talent.

They arrived at the mess room. They helped themselves to breakfast and Julie led Beth to a nearby table, where they sat alone.

'Did you like being a journalist?' asked Beth.

'It was great. But my work here isn't so different. I'm still standing up for truth and freedom. This is just a lot more …'

'Exciting?'

'Dangerous,' said Julie. 'And painful.' She bit her lip. 'You see, I have a husband and a baby.'

She paled, and rested her knife and fork on the table.

'My little girl is sixteen months old. I haven't heard from them since I arrived in this bunker five months ago. They don't even know where I am.' She brought her hand up to her forehead. 'I have no idea if they survived the invasion.'

Julie's fingers carved furrows as she dragged them backwards through her hair. Beth looked around the mess room at the other personnel - some helping themselves to hearty portions of breakfast, others chatting or joking in small groups.

'Everybody here has left someone behind,' said Julie. 'We can't even keep photos: if the cell were discovered, the Malvanians would punish our families too.'

'I've got a picture of my family in my rucksack.' As soon as she said it she realised how insensitive she was being. But Julie smiled kindly.

'I'm sorry, Beth. It would have been destroyed the moment you arrived.' She reached across the table and held Beth's hand. 'I'm afraid that standing up for what is right is a lonely business.'

Julie picked up her knife and fork and finished her breakfast without speaking. Beth chewed thoughtfully. She decided she would check her rucksack for the photo as soon as she could. She was certain that they would let her keep it, seeing as she was just a visitor.

Ricky joined them.

'Hi guys.' He sat down next to Beth.

'Hey there, what's up?' she said - then hated herself because she sounded like an idiot.

Ricky raised his eyebrows a little and tucked into his toast.

A medic called Clare sat with them and chatted to Julie. Beth noticed the colour returning to Julie's cheeks and felt relieved.

'Did you sleep OK?' Ricky asked.

She drew breath quickly, charmed by the concern in his voice. To her horror, this caused her to choke on her bacon and tomato, and a small fountain of tomato juice sprayed out of her mouth onto the table.

'Nice one,' said Ricky, passing her a paper napkin.

She felt her face blush with shame.

She continued to eat without looking up, but she could see him out of the corner of her eye. What was he doing?

Was he looking at her? Maybe he was laughing at her. She was too scared to turn and find out.

A bell rang again.

'Beth,' said Ricky.

Her legs trembled underneath the table.

'Cell Commander wants to see you. Interrogation Room One, as before.'

She couldn't tell whether he was being serious or not. She daren't speak in case it sounded stupid.

Ricky's eyes twinkled. 'My dad wants a chat with you?' he said. 'Don't worry - no thumb screws this time.'

He patted her reassuringly on the wrist. She felt her heart flip, and her eyes darted uncontrollably towards his face. He was looking straight back at her, smiling as usual. She looked away and nodded her reply in the direction of the salt pot on the table. Her cheeks stung in embarrassment and she couldn't believe she was acting like such a berk.

Ricky took her to the room where she had been questioned the day before. Ian Forsyth was waiting for her. He looked just as severe as he had yesterday, and he studied her face for some time before he spoke.

'Beth - I hope you understand just how grave the situation is for our country right now.'

She nodded.

'Yes,' continued Forsyth, 'your own family's experience has taught you that, I think. These are wretched times, Beth, and the British Resistance has to be prepared to do horrible things that no-one should normally have to do.'

'I understand all that,' said Beth, 'I promise I won't get in your way.'

'I don't think you *do* understand,' said Forsyth. 'When the hour comes to fight back against the Malvanians we *must* be ready: the consequences of a botched uprising are too dreadful to contemplate.' He paused. 'Your arrival here has created a considerable problem.'

She squirmed in her seat. She didn't like being described as a problem and she looked at Forsyth sullenly.

'It is imperative, Beth, that the British Resistance does not fail. Every member of the team must be trained in *all* the necessary skills. We cannot have a passenger holding us back.'

She felt hurt. She wasn't a little kid any more, so why was he speaking to her like that?

Forsyth read her thoughts. 'Your presence here is unfortunate. But now you *are* here, your full participation in the Resistance movement is unavoidable. It is an extremely difficult situation for us all, but in these terrible times we have no choice. We have to proceed with your training. I am now going to explain to you exactly what that means.'

She listened as Forsyth described the military initiation that lay ahead of her. She sat, paralysed, watching Forsyth's mouth open and shut. His words crashed into her ears and rebounded inside her skull until she felt sick.

***

Beth sat in the first aid room waiting for Clare the medic to give her a psychological assessment and strap up her ankle. As Clare stapled the pages of a questionnaire together and snapped them into a clipboard, Beth recalled a news report that she had seen on television. A group of young boys from Uganda were fighting in a civil war. They had no family to look after them, they were living in the shattered remains of a blown-up house, and they had no shoes. She remembered the haunted look in their eyes as they showed the reporter their weapons and talked about how many people they had killed. One of the boys was barely taller than his own machine gun. The reporter visited a rescue centre that looked after child soldiers. A boy told him that being at school was helping him cope with nightmares and flashbacks.

Beth felt a lump rise in her throat, but however much she tried she couldn't swallow it down again.

'Are you ready?' said Clare.

Beth forced herself to speak.

'I'm not sure,' she said.

Chapter Seventeen
Brave New World

Forsyth took her to the kitchen.

'Your initiation will begin now,' he said.

A man with a thick neck and shaved head was leaning over a saucepan, tasting its contents. He put the spoon down and came to meet them.

'Beth, this is Gerry Martin,' said Forsyth. 'He is our head cook and a fully trained Resistance fighter. I will leave you in his capable hands.' He nodded to Gerry and left.

'I hope you're a quick learner,' said Gerry. He wiped the sweat from his face with a napkin. 'I've got twenty-one dinners to get out by twelve.'

He walked off and Beth followed him into the store cupboard.

'Number one rule of resistance work,' he said, 'use the things around you.'

He picked up a kilo bag of sugar and dumped it in Beth's arms.

'You may find yourself in a situation where you have no military gear to help you.' He smoothed down his apron. 'Sugar is a valuable weapon. It is easily begged, borrowed or stolen. Pour some of that in a car's petrol tank and the car will grind to a halt within minutes. The engine will be wrecked beyond repair.'

He took a packet of pepper and put it on top of the sugar.

'Pepper. Throw that in somebody's eyes and they will be disabled for several minutes. Long enough for you to escape, or to continue on your mission.'

He opened the fridge door and took out a fillet of fish in a plastic bag.

'Fish,' he said, piling it on top of the sugar and pepper. 'That's somebody's dinner today so don't drop it. A piece of fish can clear a building. Hide it down the back of a warm radiator and the stink will be so bad after a couple of days that they'll be running screaming out the door.' He added a portion of mince to Beth's bundle. 'Any form of dead animal will do the job but fish is the best.'

Beth's arms were aching. Gerry put a roll of aluminium foil on the top of the pile, and she held it in place with her chin.

'Foil. Many uses. It reflects light, so can be used for signalling. It can be used to keep water out - or in. You can mould it into any shape you want and it doesn't need glue. It will keep you warm and dry at night. It conducts electricity so you can mend your torch with it if the batteries are loose.'

He shoved a jar of honey into Beth's left hand and a pot of jam into her right.

'Jam and honey attract insects. Especially wasps and ants. Might get a soldier out of his sentry post long enough for you to take advantage.'

He stared at her until she felt uncomfortable.

'Now, missy. I hope you were watching as well as listening.' He put his hands on his hips and puffed out his chest. 'I'm going to ask you to put all that back where it came from. And while you do it, you're going to tell me what you've learnt.'

Beth never had any problem memorising things, and she completed the task easily.

'Not bad,' said Gerry without smiling. 'Come back tomorrow and I'll test you again.'

He looked at his watch.

'You have to go,' he said. 'Two litres of parsley sauce won't make itself.'

He took her along a new stretch of corridor and down some stairs to a lower level. He pushed open a reinforced door that was at least twenty centimetres thick.

A man came out of a nearby room. He had sandy hair and freckled skin.

'This is Mick Robson,' said Gerry. 'He's our explosives expert.'

He returned to the kitchen.

Robson shook Beth's hand and indicated that she should sit down. There was a lunch box in the middle of the table. Robson peeled back the lid and took out what looked like a lump of uncooked pastry, about the size of his fist.

'This is plastic explosive,' he said. 'Sometimes it will be necessary to force our way into buildings, and blowing a hole in a wall can be an effective way to do this.'

He handed it to Beth. It felt cold to the touch.

'Can I squeeze it?' she said.

'Go ahead. You need to feel comfortable handling it.'

'What's it made of?'

'A tried and tested compound known as C4.'

She pressed into the surface and her fingers left four deep imprints.

'We may be required to blow up railway lines and bridges,' said Robson. 'Anything that weakens Malvanian transport and communication routes.' He leaned forward. 'A piece that small could easily destroy a section of train track.'

Beth put the lump to her nose and sniffed it.

Robson eyed her seriously and continued. 'We sometimes have to plant explosives in vehicles and buildings. Sometimes - we have to kill the people inside them.'

She dropped the beige lump in disgust, then screamed as it landed on the table, fearing that the impact would make it explode. Robson picked it up.

'In this state, it is stable and harmless,' he said. 'It needs to be rendered active. You will not have to do this yourself, but I will show you how it is done. Then I will teach you how to conceal a device and detonate it.'

He stood up and patted her shoulder.

'Before that, please wash your hands.'

***

Julie joined her at lunch.

'Eat well while you can,' she said. 'Some of our field training exercises last all day.'

Beth stopped shoving her food round her plate and tried to chew some of it.

'That's more like it,' said Julie.

'I can't swallow,' said Beth.

Julie pushed a bowl of cherry pie and tinned cream across the table towards her.

'At least have this. Come on, you know you want to!'

It was definitely easier to eat. When she had finished Julie took her back to the lower level of the bunker.

Forsyth met her and showed her into another room.

'This is where we practice using firearms,' he said.

There were two identical guns lying side by side on a table. Forsyth picked one of them up.

'This is the SIG Sauer P229 pistol. It has a lighter, smoother action than most handguns and is therefore ideal for use by civilians. Its compact size means it can be easily hidden under clothing.'

He placed it flat on his hand.

'I am going to give it to you and show you how to hold it. At the moment it is not loaded. Nevertheless, do not point it at yourself, do not point it at me. Do not point it at anyone who might enter the room. When I give the order, you will point it only at the target I specify. Understood?'

Beth took the pistol. It was surprisingly heavy. Forsyth showed her how to handle it, naming each component in turn.

'Good.' He picked up a small, rectangular box. 'This contains thirteen rounds. Bullets. We call it a 'clip'. We insert it into handle of the pistol - thus.'

He showed her how to put the clip in and remove it again.

'I will now demonstrate the capability of this weapon. Please stand behind the table.'

He walked forward and fired several rounds into a sandbag at the other end of the room.

'Come and have a look,' he said.

Beth walked to the sandbag. It was slumped forwards, sand weeping from the bullet holes into a yellow pool on the floor.

Forsyth replaced the sandbag and they returned to the table. There was a rich, metallic click as Forsyth removed the empty clip from his gun.

'Now it's your turn.'

Under Forsyth's guidance, Beth loaded her weapon, took aim and fired. She felt a strong kick travel up her arms and into her torso. She steadied herself, and fired again. And again, until the clip had been discharged.

At the other end of the room, the sandbag bled until it was empty.

***

Ricky was waiting for her outside the door.

'Keep smiling, soldier girl!' he said. 'You're doing great.'

He smelled of soap. Sort of spicy and clean at the same time.

'You've got me for your next training session,' he said. 'But you'll need to get changed into your civvies. Your normal clothes. Meet me on 'B' corridor in ten minutes.'

She nodded.

'You are allowed to talk to me, you know!'

He smiled; she blushed again. They parted company and Beth headed for the sleeping quarters.

Once changed, she met him as agreed. He opened a hatch and led her down a long, dimly lit tunnel. At the other end was a small door. He pushed it open and sunlight flooded onto his face and shimmered in his hair.

'Mind out,' he said.

They pushed through a thicket of nettles, and Beth found herself standing by a barn. There was an old Land Rover parked nearby. In the distance, a delivery truck arrived at a farmhouse. Hundreds of sheep were scattered like woolly pebbles over the sloping fields.

'Welcome to Farley Farm,' said Ricky. 'The whole bunker is built under the farmer's land. He is a supporter of our work and he'll cover for us if any Malvanians turn up.'

He gave her some fake ID and travel papers. 'It won't happen - but if it does, you'll need these. You are Kelly, the farmer's niece. I'm his nephew David. We're visiting the farm for a few days to help out.'

He was wearing jeans and a blue checked shirt, and it made him look more like a boy, not a soldier.

'Why are we here?' She felt much more comfortable wearing her own clothes and talking to him felt easy.

'Driving lesson.' He walked over to the Land Rover and opened the door. 'Come on, get in.'

She sat in the driver's seat. Ricky showed her how to adjust the seat and mirrors, and what the pedals were for.

'Now put your seat belt on. Turn the ignition key to start the engine. That's right.'

The engine chugged noisily.

'Someday you might have to start a car without the key. I'll show you how another time. For now, you must learn to drive properly so you don't draw attention to yourself on the roads. We can do the crazy stuff later.'

She followed Ricky's instructions, and soon the Land Rover moved forwards. She drove round the yard for several metres before the engine stalled and they came to an abrupt stop.

She covered her face with her hands. 'Oh no, I'm rubbish!'

'That was amazing for a first go,' said Ricky. He put the gear stick back into 'neutral'. 'Don't be so shy with the accelerator pedal next time. You'll be fine.'

They spent the afternoon driving around the yard, and then along the dirt track that ran around the outskirts of the farm, the wheels of the Land Rover sending a stream of dust into the summer air. It got easier with every attempt - and Beth felt relaxed and free as she drove slowly up and down, the sun soaking into her skin and the fragrant smell of grass and animals floating in through the open windows.

'Stop here,' said Ricky.

She brought the car to a halt and put on the handbrake. They were right at the top of the farm, and the sheep in the farthest fields looked no bigger than fluffy grains of rice.

Ricky looked at his watch.

'Nearly time to go back,' he said. 'You've got a Malvanian lesson with Dyche this evening. Let's do one more circuit and get you driving in third gear. You'll have to go a bit faster.'

It was a little cooler now, and delicate breeze brushed her skin as she drove back towards the barn. The track ran downhill, and this time she allowed the Land Rover to gather speed as it descended the slope.

'Now!' said Ricky. 'Take her into third!'

The tyres seemed to grip the road harder, and they lurched forward. The breeze got into Beth's hair and it made her feel a little wild. She pressed the accelerator harder and the dust flew out of the track around them. She liked the new noise the engine made; her shirt fluttered on her skin; a hint of Ricky's spicy soap tickled her nostrils and her heart rate increased. This was fantastic!

The front wheel struck something hard in the road and the Land Rover kicked violently. Stupidly, she pressed the accelerator instead of the brake and lost control of the wheel. They swerved off the track and landed in a ditch. The seatbelt grazed her collarbone as she lunged forward, then jarred backwards in her seat.

Ricky got out and inspected the front of the vehicle, bending down for a moment to pull a load of weeds out of the gap between the bumper and the grille.

'She's stuck,' he called.

He returned to the front passenger seat.

'Well now, little miss soldier girl …' He spoke in a funny accent and pretended he was reading off a clipboard. 'I'm afraid you have failed your driving test. You made just one, tiny mistake …'

Beth felt a smile creep across her face. Ricky nudged her and laughed.

'Here.' He had picked a large daisy from the grass and he playfully brushed the petals against her arm. The early evening air ruffled his hair and her heart danced inside her. She took the daisy, their fingers not quite touching as she clasped the fragile stalk.

***

After supper Beth went to her sleeping quarters. She lay on her bed, reliving the day's events. She wished she could tell her dad where she was and what she was doing - he would be so proud of her. And Peter would go berserk if he knew that she had handled bombs and learnt to fire a real gun. Most of all she wanted to talk to her mum about the wonderful new boy she had met, and hear her soft, calm voice give her the advice she needed.

But a phone call was out of the question; she understood that now. She reached for her rucksack and felt inside the front pocket. It would be nice to see a picture of them at least. She searched the main cavity and all the other pockets - twice.

The family photo wasn't there.

Of course it wasn't. Julie had been right.

She closed her eyes as tightly as she could and tried to bring back a perfect image of the day the photo was taken. Curling up on the bed, she fell asleep with her boots on.

Chapter Eighteen
Child - Adult - Child

The evening sun was the colour of blood. Beth zig-zagged through the wood, using the trees as cover, her gun poised to defend herself. The trees gave way to long grass and she continued her journey on her stomach, inching forward using her knees and elbows. She was nearly there. From the east she heard the rhythmic clatter of heavy wheels speeding along a railway track. She paused until the train had passed. Then, every fibre of muscle in her body hurting, she pulled herself forwards again.

There was a low whistle, and she stopped. She rested her face on her arm and tried to get her breath back. There was a movement in the grass and Forsyth drew alongside her. His eyeballs stood out like hard-boiled eggs against the dark camouflage paint on his face. He opened his mouth to speak and his teeth, too, looked freakishly white.

'Well done,' he said.

He whistled again - twice, this time, and signalled to Beth that she should crawl back to the woods. Her elbows felt raw as she dug them into the hard earth, and drips of sweat fell from her face and left chocolate-coloured marks in the dust. She was glad when she reached the trees, and vigorously massaged her shoulders and lower back when she stood up. Forsyth was soon at her side again. Ahead of them, through the trees, pairs of Resistance personnel were making their way back to the bunker: one in front, their partner covering their back. After fifty metres or so, the person at the rear would overtake their colleague and the roles were reversed. Beth and Forsyth followed the same routine and were the last to reach the bunker.

Inside, she leant against the wall and looked at her watch. The exercise had lasted nine hours. She couldn't wait to have a shower, eat a hot meal and go to sleep.

'Good work, people,' said Forsyth. 'There will be a debriefing in two hours. Get yourselves cleaned up and fed.' He walked away.

Julie caught her eye from the other side of the room and mouthed:

'You all right?'

She smiled feebly.

Ricky looked over and gave her the thumbs up - and her heart melted. Her strength returned and she walked towards him. She longed to sit shoulder to shoulder with him at supper and listen to his jokes.

'Beth, please would you come with me?'

It was Wally Dyche. He led her away from the group and through the bunker until they were back at the room where she had been questioned on her first day. Dyche opened the door for her: Forsyth was waiting inside.

She smiled and sat down.

There was a large tray on the desk, covered with a tea

towel. Without speaking, Forsyth took the tea towel away. On the tray were a bunch of keys, a Swiss army knife, somebody's old diary, a book of matches, a family photograph taken at a party, a car number plate, a pair of shoes and a mobile phone.

'You have five minutes to memorise what is on this tray,' said Forsyth.

He could at least have complimented her! She had worked really hard today, and she thought he was being pretty mean. But she knew this task would be easy for her. She didn't need anywhere near five minutes to do it, even though she was very tired. Long before the time was up she had memorised everything, and to stop herself getting bored, she had learnt the numbers on the number plate and the address of the hotel featured on the book of matches. Forsyth replaced the tea towel.

'Tell me what is on the tray,' he said.

'Keys - knife - photo - diary - matches - number plate - phone - shoes. The number plate was LZ04 ITM. The matches came from the Swan Hotel, Monksford, MD17 4HY.'

'How many keys were there?'

'Six, I think.'

'You *think*? Not good enough.'

Why was he being so picky?

'Tell me about the knife.'

'It's brown ... or dark red.'

'Which?'

'Dark red.'

'Lucky guess. How many matches were left inside the book?'

'I don't know.'

'Of course you don't. You didn't look. You had five minutes to find out - and you didn't look.'

He tapped his forefinger on the desk.

'Whose diary was it?' He looked impatient. 'I'll answer that for you: You don't know. Let's go back to the number plate. Tell me more: was it from the front of the back of a car?'

How was she supposed to know that?

'All cars have white plates at the front and yellow at the back.'

'I'm sorry, I didn't notice.' Her words came out in a tearful whisper.

Forsyth banged his hand on the desk. He lifted the tea towel.

'I will repeat my instructions to you.' He shook his head as he spoke. 'You have five minutes to memorise *what is on the tray.*'

Her hurt turned to anger and, seized with determination, she picked up each item, examining it and making a mental note of as much detail as she could. She ignored her hunger, her thirst - the throbbing in her head and the extreme heaviness in her body. She didn't understand why she was being made to do this, but she knew that Forsyth would not let her go until she completed the task to his satisfaction.

After five minutes he asked her to tell him what she had remembered.

'A bunch of six keys; five silver, one gold-ish. Of the silver ones, four look like front door keys, one is small and looks like it's for a shed or garage. The gold one is like a second lock for a front door.'

'What about the keyring?'

'Green leather, with a 'K' on it in gold.'

'So who owns these keys?'

'A man?'

Forsyth's eyes said he needed more.

'Er, not a flashy guy, quite normal, and not young. Old.' She knew she was just making this up. 'The Swiss army knife has a large knife - the small knife has been broken off - a corkscrew, things that look like blunt knives with lumps taken out, scissors, tweezers and a thin, pointy thing ...'

Forsyth raised his eyebrows disapprovingly.

'... The photo is of a mother, father and two grown-up sons.' She described their appearance and what they were wearing. 'They seem to be in their own house, because they look comfy and happy. The mobile phone is small and yellow, so probably owned by a girl. There are text messages from a boy called Jake. From the content he must be her boyfriend. I didn't have time to look at all of it, but ...' Her voice became apologetic: 'There are two names and numbers I looked at and remembered.'

She looked at Forsyth, searching for his approval. She told him the phone numbers, and that the shoes were men's size seven and they were muddy. She had looked at the diary last, and was only able to recall the name and address of its owner. Finally she said that the number plate was from the rear of a car, and that there were only two matches left in the book.

She leant back in her chair and folded her arms, hoping Forsyth would be impressed.

'Not good enough.'

Tears welled up in her eyes. Forsyth ignored it.

'Beth, you may only have five minutes in a building before you have to flee. You have to bring back maximum information.'

He turned the shoes over.

'Look: this mud is reddish colour. The soil around here is grey - so where has this man been?' He rattled the keys. 'You say there are 'four front door keys'. No - this one is thinner and with a square top. Probably opens a patio door. The fourth key bears the brand name of a company who makes security doors for airports.'

He pointed at the photo.

'See how alike the two sons are to their mother? Yet the father's features bear no resemblance. He is not a blood relative. They are all raising their glasses in a toast - it is obvious that the older son is left-handed. On the coffee table in front of them is a fifth glass of champagne, and half a cigarette is smouldering in an ashtray. Both have lipstick marks on them. They belong to the woman who is taking the picture. Look behind them: sports trophies, including two from a gun club. All this information could prove vital in assessing our enemies.'

Beth wiped her nose on her sleeve.

'Again,' said Forsyth.

'I'm too tired. I can't concentrate any more.'

Forsyth leaned forward until his face was a few centimetres from hers.

'You have to perform under pressure. The lives of the British people are in our hands. Their future freedom depends on our ability to be the best we can, however bad we feel.'

He banged on the table again.

'You have five minutes,' he said. 'Begin.'

***

Nearly two hours had passed.

'I must debrief the others,' said Forsyth.

Beth rubbed her eyes and a mixture of camouflage paint and tears came off on her hands.

'Well done,' he said. For the first time, he touched her kindly. 'I have to be tough with you, Beth. I hope you understand.'

It was difficult to hold back, but she was not going to cry in front of him again.

'You are excused from the debrief. Instead, you should shower and eat. I will give you a personal debriefing later, and Clare will be present too. You may go. You should be enormously proud of yourself.'

She left the room and fled to her sleeping quarters.

Julie was inside, putting on a fresh pair of socks. When she saw Beth she stood up.

'Oh, you poor, brave, thing,' she said.

'It's been quite a difficult day, actually,' Beth stammered, trying to sound breezy and failing miserably.

'Hug?' said Julie.

Beth launched herself into Julie's arms and sobbed like a baby.

Chapter Nineteen
Good Neighbour, Bad Neighbour

Jane stood at the sink in Mr Jafary's kitchen, washing up after lunch. Mr Jafary came in, took a plastic bucket out of the kitchen cupboard and found some cleaning cloths and a bottle of bleach.

'You're supposed to be resting,' said Jane.

Doug was out in the porch painting a brand new front door, and he called along the hallway.

'I hope you're telling him he's meant to be resting!'

'You are good friends,' said Mr Jafary. He nursed his ribs with one hand. 'They ache even when I sit still,' he said, 'so I may as well be busy.'

'Are you sure, Mohinder?' she said. 'I'll do it for you as soon as I've finished this.'

She waved a saucer covered in foam, and Mr Jafary regarded it sadly, reflecting on the fate of his prized porcelain collection.

'No, my dear,' he said, 'I need to do something. Then they haven't beaten me, you see.'

He pressed his hands together, palms facing, and made a gesture of thanks. He picked up the bucket and went into the hallway. A few moments later, Jane heard him walking slowly up the stairs.

When she finished the washing up she hurried into the hall.

'Mustn't forget the recycling,' she said. 'We don't want Mohinder to get a hundred Euro fine.'

'Absolutely not.' Doug prodded angrily at the door with his brush. 'They've taken far too much from him already.'

Jane took a bin bag from the cupboard under the stairs and went to the front door. On the other side of the street, Harold Stone was standing at an upstairs window, watching them.

'He's been there for forty-five minutes,' said Doug. 'Do you think Phyllis has super-glued him to the carpet?'

The Stone's living room curtain moved to one side and Phyllis peeped out, but as soon as she saw the Hardys she backed out of sight. Jane walked round to the side of the house and sorted the rubbish into the correct bins. When she returned to the porch, Harold was still watching them.

She went back inside, urging Doug to get the new front door finished as quickly as possible.

***

Phyllis scurried away from the living room window and into the kitchen. Some fruit scones were cooking in the oven, and she breathed in the rich, sweet fumes. Baking always made her feel good: it was how she met Harold. She would never forget the day he complimented her on her Victoria sponge.

'Did you make that yourself?' he had asked, when she served him with tea and cake at a village fete thirty-two years ago.

She blushed and said 'yes'.

'Well, well,' he said, casting his eyes over her dull clothes and spindly body, 'you'll make some fellow a useful wife, I'm sure.'

Phyllis had been paid so few compliments in her life that she was greatly flattered. Fifteen minutes later she summed up her courage, walked over to his table and offered him another slice of cake, free of charge.

'Don't mind if I do,' said Harold, regarding first the piece of cake - and then Phyllis - with increased interest. 'Any chance of another cup of tea as well...you know, on the house?'

Phyllis brought him a second cup of tea; Harold licked his lips, and their relationship began.

The oven timer pinged. Phyllis opened the door and an intoxicating smell flooded into the kitchen. She forgot all about Mr Jafary's house and hummed to herself as she placed the scones on a wire rack to cool. Harold would stop being cross with her now. She put some strawberry jam in a pot and opened a cupboard in search of the butter dish.

***

Upstairs, Stone moved away from the window and returned to his computer to smirk at the e-mail which had arrived from the Malvanian authorities:

!!GRAND-AKOMPLISCHMENTZ
SIGNOR HAROLD STONE!!
CONGRATULATIONS MR HAROLD STONE!

You are our 10,000th informant.

You have won a special trip to London at our expense.

As he re-read it for the umpteenth time, the 'you've got mail' icon flashed again. There was another message from the Ministry of Informants. It began:

'*METHODICKEN VUR KOVERTISCH INFOSNATCHEN UND NEEBORSCHNOOPEN.*
Ways to Gather Information and
Spy on Your Neighbours.'

He was about to press 'Print' when he heard Phyllis coming up the stairs. He changed the screen to a website about vintage cars, and was reading it avidly when she entered the room. He picked up one of the scones, placed it on a plate and cut it in half. He slowly buttered it, and the butter sank slowly into the soft, warm floury dough. Phyllis smiled nervously at him as he dripped a dollop of sticky red jam from the spoon. He lifted the scone portion to his mouth and took a large bite. Phyllis let out a long breath in relief. But it was too soon. Harold spat the scone out onto the tray, where it lay in a half-chewed blob.

'Too much fruit, you silly cow,' he said. 'You know I hate it when there's too much ruddy fruit.'

He stood up and smashed the tray on to the floor with a single sweep of his hand. Phyllis, flapping like a tiny bird, moved forward to tidy it up, but he raised his hand again. Phyllis went flying and she landed with a thud, face down amongst the tea things.

Chapter Twenty
Turnaround

Beth stood in front of the washroom mirror and wiped the remaining smears of camouflage paint from her face. As she pulled a clean khaki vest over her head she watched her sinewy muscles flexing and releasing. She walked to her bed and cleaned her boots. With deft strokes of the brush she flicked away bits of grass and mud. She watched the dirt particles join the dust floating in the air and reflected on the past eighteen days. At times she had wanted to scream and beg to be taken home - but the team had always been there to instruct and encourage her. Ricky had been brilliant. He had been by her side throughout. A thrill fluttered in her chest when she thought about him: his light blond hair, his golden tanned skin and his mischievous smile. And his strong arms and muscly legs. And his deep voice and that nice sweaty smell. And his gorgeous blue eyes. And his toned, masculine chest ...

The dinner bell rang. She spat on the toe of her boot and vigorously brought it to a high sheen. She put on the boots, rearranged her fringe and pinched her cheeks to bring some colour to her face. Then she headed for the mess room. She strode along the corridor, a feeling of fitness and strength surging through her legs as she moved forward.

At the end of the corridor she noticed one of the doors was open. Inside, Ricky was slumped in a chair with his back to her, feet up on the table, listening to music on his MP3 player. He was singing to himself and pretending to play the drums.

'Oi, Mr Rock Star!' she said, 'shouldn't you be doing that in the common room? And get your fat feet off the table!'

He didn't hear her, so she raised her voice.

'You look like a gibbon and you sound like a bulldog with laryngitis!'

He bashed out a flamboyant riff on the cymbals and Beth snorted with laughter. She went up behind him and tapped him on the shoulder. He scrambled upright, pulling his legs off the table and plucking the earphones out of his ears.

'Enjoying yourself?' said Beth.

'Jeez, I thought you were my dad,' he said.

'I know.' She tilted her head a little, challenging him to tell her off.

'Bad girl,' he said, jumping out of his chair and grabbing her in a headlock, 'try and get out of this!'

She squealed and stamped on his foot.

'That's rubbish!' he said, still holding her in the headlock with one arm and patting her on the forehead with his other hand. She was laughing so much that she had no strength at all, and he started dragging her round the room.

'Come on, weakling - surrender!'

'Never!'

She seized his little finger and bent it over backwards. He recoiled in pain and surprise, but before he could regain his balance, she rammed her hand into his throat and pushed him backwards, pinning him against the wall. His head clunked against the bricks, and she looked up at him breathlessly.

'I won't do the next bit,' she said, flexing her free fist and preparing to propel her knee into his groin. She kept hold of his throat and maintained eye contact.

'Question is, do *you* surrender?' she said.

She could feel the heat coming off his body, his bare skin was sweaty underneath her fingers, and the artery in his neck was pulsating. She had never been this close to a boy before and it felt glorious. She felt no shyness, no need to break her gaze. She raised her eyebrows at him. He smiled and unpeeled her hand from his throat.

'Looks like I surrender,' he said softly.

He couldn't stop looking at her. Her head was spinning and she could actually hear bells ringing in her ears. She kept her eyes fixed on his face and curled her fingers around his a little. He tightened his grip in return and moved his lips towards hers.

Suddenly his expression changed and he tossed her hand away in embarrassment. Casually, he walked away from her, towards the table where he'd left the MP3 player. He seemed to rebuke himself under his breath, and fiddled with the earphones for several seconds before turning to face her again.

'Dinner time, kiddo,' he said, and stalked out of the room.

She followed him down the corridor and into the mess room, where they parted company. They sat on different tables with their backs to each other, and after dinner, Ricky cleared his plates as soon as possible and left the room. She watched him leave, pushing the remains of a barely-touched steak and kidney pie around her plate, and wondering what on earth had just happened to her.

***

She was having a nightmare. She tried to shout but she moaned strangely instead. Forcing her eyes open, she kicked off the bedclothes. In the darkness she could hear Julie breathing and the low drone of the air conditioning system. She rubbed her face, got up, felt her way to the bathroom, filled a glass of water from the tap and drank it. The horror of the dream was clinging to her like a damp blanket, so she walked out through the dormitory and into the corridor where the lights were on. She wandered towards the Operations Room, trying to wake herself up and banish the bad dream for good.

As she walked, she thought she could hear voices coming from one of the smaller rooms. The door was ajar, so she stood outside and listened. It was Commander Forsyth and Ricky.

'I must admit that I am surprised at how capable she is,' said Forsyth. 'She has shown great resilience and has learnt quickly. My fears that her presence here would compromise the mission have proved, largely, to be unfounded.'

'Exactly,' said Ricky.

'But she is still a liability. She's just a kid, for God's sake. You may well find it a pain in the backside to shadow her all the time, but it is *absolutely* necessary.'

'I'm sick of being a babysitter,' Ricky said. 'Julie's really good with her - can't she be nanny for a bit?'

'No,' said Forsyth. 'You have your orders, and you will carry them out like a soldier.'

'Soldier!' said Ricky. 'Exactly – I'm a soldier, not a stupid, blinking wet nurse. I didn't join the Resistance so I could play Barbies with the cute kid from the kindergarten!'

A chair clattered to the ground.

'I'd stop there right now,' said Forsyth. 'One more word and I will punish you for insubordination.'

Beth did not hear Ricky's reply. She turned and ran along the corridor.

Back in the darkened dormitory, she dressed and packed her rucksack. She turned Ricky's words over in her head. How could she have been so stupid? He didn't care about her, he was just following orders. All that smiling and twinkly eyes – he was just laughing at her because he thought she was a dumb kid. She felt around in the bedside cabinet for Jackson, and shoved him into one of the side pockets of the backpack. Then she remembered the way that Ricky had looked at her before dinner. She recalled his fingers lightly touching hers, and she felt a soft frisson of pain run up her spine. Then his words came again to haunt her, and a white-hot flash of indignation consumed her. How could he?

'I am not a ruddy child!' she muttered. She looked at Julie and wondered if she, too, was only caring for her because Forsyth had told her to. Maybe they *all* thought she was just an annoying kid.

A flush of determination radiated upwards from her chest into her face.

'Let's see who's the useless kid, then, shall we?'

She lifted the backpack onto her shoulders. She crept out of the dormitory and flitted through the corridors until she came to a fire exit. Without looking back, she depressed the door release bar, opened the door and disappeared into the night.

PART TWO

Chapter Twenty-One
Transformation

On the outskirts of a village just outside the M25, a Malvanian soldier on night patrol stopped to light a cigarette. He stared vacantly at the hedge in front of him and clicked his lighter repeatedly, trying to get a spark. Finally he lost patience, swore under his breath, threw the defunct lighter into the foliage and fumbled in his pockets for a box of matches.

The lighter struck Beth in the midriff. She was standing no more than a metre away from the soldier, regarding him silently from amongst the leaves. She had been watching him for four consecutive nights, and knew that his name was Freddie. As he struck a match and sucked the first nicotine fumes into his lungs, a young woman appeared at the far end of the road. She waved at him, trying to keep her stilettoed footsteps quiet. Beth knew her name too: Tracy.

Freddie lost interest in his cigarette, licked his finger and used it to smooth down his hair, eyeing his girlfriend's legs as they tottered along the pavement towards him. Beth glanced at her watch: Tracy was five minutes late tonight. Freddie crossed the road. The couple embraced; he crooned something to her in a low voice and she giggled. She took hold of his hand and led him down the street into an old wooden bus shelter. They disappeared inside. There was another giggle, then silence. Beth waited for a few minutes. Then she parted the leaves of the hedge and moved silently down the street in the opposite direction.

Minutes later she walked anonymously past a series of large, detached houses - and one with no lights on caught her eye. She stopped and ran a reconnaissance checklist through her head:

- all windows closed, despite it being a warm, humid night - check.
- no sign of burglar alarm - check.
- letters and newspapers piling up on the front doormat - check.
- no gravel on the driveway - check.
- no car in the drive; garage door obstructed by undisturbed garden debris - check.
- no one watching - check.

She grasped the front gate and propelled herself over the top of it. Ducking behind a shrub, she scanned the house for security lights: there was one set up to illuminate the path to the back door. She walked towards the light, removed her camouflage cap, took aim and sent it looping into the air like a Frisbee. It landed on the light, blocking the detector, and she darted down the side of the house. At the back was a single-storey kitchen extension with a flat roof; above it was the bathroom. She took hold of the drainpipe and gave it a tug to see if it was secure, then she climbed athletically. Crouching on the kitchen roof, she snapped an army knife from the clip on her belt, selected a long, thin flexible blade and moved towards the bathroom window. She stood up, and felt carefully around the perimeter of both window panels. The small, upper window was loose. She inserted the knife between the window and its frame and manipulated the blade until she had worked it into the latch mechanism. With a sharp twist she forced the latch open and pushed her arm down through the gap, searching for the handle of the larger window.

A portion of the broken latch fell off and tumbled into the bathroom sink, bouncing round the enamel bowl. She lunged helplessly towards it, but it was out of arm's reach, and it orbited the plughole in noisy circles. She looked back over her shoulder and, as the chunk of metal bobbled at the bottom of the sink, she heard the clicking of dog claws on the patio in the adjoining garden.

The dog sniffed the air and started barking. It hurled itself repeatedly at the fence, scratching at the fence posts and grinding its teeth. Quickly she withdrew her hand from the window, rolled across the roof to the other side of the kitchen and dropped onto the lawn below. Hiding behind a wheelbarrow, she despatched the soft, bendy blade back into the body of the knife. She flicked out a razor-sharp hunting dagger, assumed a defensive position and listened. The dog continued to strike the fence with the full force of its body, its bark burbling in its own saliva.

A light went on at the back of the house next door and the owner came out into the garden. He flashed a torch over the fence but could see nothing.

'Who's a daft little Chipper Sausage! They're not there, are they?'

Chipper whimpered like a bashful guinea pig, and the man led the dog indoors, reprimanding it for being a 'fuzzy-fuss-pot'. The light went off again, and Beth climbed back onto the roof. She squeezed her arm inside the small window for the second time, opened the larger one and climbed into the bathroom. She closed both windows behind her and moved from room to room inside the house, double-checking that there was nobody at home. There was a telephone on a table in the hall, and she listened to the messages through the handset:

'Hey Lucy! Hope your hols were really cool! Did you get me one of those African bracelets? Give me a call when you get back!'

'Steve - it's Peter Cardew. Had a bit of a crisis at the board meeting. Tried your mobile but I guess you're out of range. Call me ASAP.'

'Hi Jen it's me. Would Rupert and Harry like to come round for tea the day after you get home? Josh has really missed them.'

'Darling? Hello? - It's Mum. We're watching the news. Something dreadful seems to be happening, soldiers everywhere, we can't … Call us, please?'

Beth replaced the receiver and switched on a torch. Sitting on the bottom stair, she opened and read all the mail on the doormat. She sifted through the filing cabinet in the office and raided the kitchen drawers.

She logged her findings in her head: holiday brochures, receipts, bank statements, household bills and personal letters. This family had gone on safari to Kenya in May but had not returned home after the invasion. She went back into the kitchen and made one final check: that there was no cat's bowl on the floor and no animal food of any kind in the cupboards. She didn't want to be discovered by the man next door coming in to feed a pet. She walked upstairs and into a bedroom, lay down on the bed and fell asleep.

When she awoke, still clutching her army knife, the sun was shining in a bright halo round the edge of the curtains. She got up and made a second sweep of the house from top to bottom; then she returned to the bedroom and continued her search for information. There was a poster of the cast of an American teen musical on the wall, a pin board covered in photos taken at a Year Twelve disco: girls hugging each other and groups of boys showing off, and enough cuddly toys to open a synthetic zoo.

She switched on the computer. In the top drawer of the desk was a sequinned address book. She turned to the back page and found a list of passwords written in purple gel pen. She spent an hour trawling through e-mails and reading Tweets, then she rifled through a folder full of school reports and exam certificates. She returned to the computer and memorised maps and satellite images of the local area. Then she went downstairs. The photographs in the living room confirmed that this was the Marshall family: Jen and Steve, and their children Rupert, Harry and Lucy. Beth studied the photos of Lucy carefully. Short, blonde hair and a big grin. The picture of her standing at the bottom of a cliff wearing abseiling gear showed that Lucy had a taste for adventure. Just the sort of girl who might want to join a Malvanian Youth camp, in fact.

A holiday snap of Jen standing in front of the Eiffel Tower caught her eye. Jen had blonde hair like Lucy – but the Parisian sunshine exposed her dark roots. Beth picked up the photo of Lucy, went back upstairs and into Steve and Jen's en-suite bathroom. She searched the cupboards until she found what she was looking for: Jen's hair bleaching kit.

'Are you a vivacious blonde trapped inside a bored brunette? Unlock your Real Self with this easy-to-use home hair lightening kit.

You won't regret it!'

Using a pair of nail scissors, she cut her hair into the same, cropped style that Lucy wore. She followed the instructions on the side of the bleaching kit. Then she sat on the bathroom floor and waited for forty minutes before rinsing her hair and towelling it dry. She looked in the mirror: a muscular, gritty-eyed blonde girl was staring back at her. She could easily be seventeen. She bent down and scooped up the pile of light brown hair from the bathroom floor. It felt dry and dead already, as if it had never been hers. She stuffed it into a polythene bag, walked downstairs and into the kitchen. She dropped the bag into the kitchen bin and let the lid swing shut. Then she raided the cupboards and the freezer for brunch.

Chapter Twenty-Two
Application

Three pork chops, baked beans, tinned tomatoes and several slices of toast later, Beth sat at the kitchen table drinking a mug of black coffee with three sugars. A twelve page A4 booklet was spread in front of her:

APPLICAZION VOR ZEE ACTIVITEE
KAMPS OB ZEE
YUZE MALVANISCH.
Application Form for Malvanian Youth Camps.

She wrote 'Lucy Jane Marshall' at the top of the first page, and filled in the address. She copied out Lucy's school details and exam results. Page two asked for her medical records. She would need to find the relevant documents in the filing cabinet, and decided to look for them later. She turned to page three.

VOR UNIFORM – FITTINGS

There was a complex chart, asking for every possible measurement, including the circumference of her head for her *Flünken* helmet. She found a tape measure and filled in each box as requested.

Page four said:

SPILLEN OND ZEENEN & DUREN FAMILEE:
Tell Us About You and Your Family!

Have you had any detentions at school?
Have you been to a music festival?
Have you ever been on a protest march?
Do you like cricket?
Has your daddy ever made jokes about the
Malvanian army?
Does your mummy still bake those lovely
English cakes you like to eat?
Do you like Smit the Clown? Do your parents
like him?
Has Granny or Grandad got any Royal
Family souvenirs?

She felt the hairs prick up on the back of her neck, and wondered how many children had betrayed their families to the Malvanian Authorities by innocently answering these questions. She swallowed a mouthful of coffee and flicked the pen between her fingers. This was going to take her some time.

That night, she let herself out of the Marshalls' back door, walked up the garden path and vaulted over the gate. She was dressed in Lucy's blue and grey striped sweatshirt, jeans and had a navy baseball cap pulled down over her face. She headed for the train station. As she turned the corner at the end of the road, she saw a man who was tinkering with his car under a street lamp.

He caught his hand on something and swore loudly.

'Excuse my French,' he said. 'All right, love?'

Beth returned with a cheerful 'Hiya', but she kept her head down. As she walked away, she could hear that the man did not return to his work immediately. Was he watching her? Did he know Lucy? She would have to return to the house via a different route.

As she approached the station, a group of soldiers bristled to attention. She smiled at them and made eye contact.

'State your purpose,' said one of the guards.

She showed him her application form.

'I want to join the Malvanian Youth,' she said, 'but I need a photograph or I can't go.'

The soldier made a hostile gesture with his gun. 'You cannot pass without the proper papers,' he said.

'But I can't get the papers unless I have a photo! Please let me go in!'

She opened her eyes as widely as she could, and a second soldier spoke.

'*En eez vur zee Yude Malvanisch!*' he said to his colleague. 'I will watch her. Then there is no harm, yes?' It was Freddie.

The first soldier narrowed his eyes. 'Very well,' he said.

Beth sat down inside the booth and removed the baseball cap. She fluffed up her hair and put the money in the slot. She could see Freddie's big feet just the other side of the curtain, rocking from heel to toe and, as the camera flashed, she heard him click out a cheery rhythm on the butt of his gun with his fingernails. What a goof, she thought. She left the booth and waited for the photographs to be developed. Freddie smiled as she pulled back the curtain, whilst the other guards scrutinised her through the foyer window. There was a whirring sound, and a sheet of four identical photos dropped out of the chute. Beth picked them up and waved them about to dry them off.

'Thank you!' she said, donned the baseball cap and left. As she walked away, the first soldier entered the foyer and made a thorough search of the photo booth.

'Nothing. *Nilsch,*' he said.

'Of course!' said Freddie.

Beth walked along the footpath that ran parallel to the railway line. The path led to the village green, and from there she could approach the Marshall's house without having to pass the man mending his car.

The green had completely changed. On the satellite photos it was a beautiful, leafy space. Now, all that remained of the sports pavilion was a flight of weed-ridden steps leading to a rotting wooden floor. The boarded-up toilet block was barely visible over a tangled thicket of hogweed. The children's play area had been torn out of the ground leaving a couple of metal stumps, from which the last flakes of coloured paint hung like sleeping moths. The cricket pitch had been cut off from the rest of the ground by a chain-link fence. She moved towards it and peered through the mesh. Two dozen pristine Malvanian army jeeps stood silently in rows of six, ready for action.

She walked away and sat on a wooden bench. Unkempt vegetation had grown through the gaps in the seat, almost to her own height. She attached her photos to the Malvanian Youth application form with a paper clip and put the form in its envelope. As she sealed the flap, she was distracted by a noise coming from inside the enclosure.

She looked over: deep within the gloom, a hooded figure was moving. She jumped over the back of the bench and lay flat in the overgrowth, watching the prowler through the plant stalks. They moved from vehicle to vehicle, pausing at the rear of each one, and eventually they reached a jeep near to the fence. They unscrewed the petrol cap and tipped a substance into the petrol tank. In the residual light the substance glinted white, and Beth knew it was the petrol engine's worst enemy: sugar.

The saboteur withdrew back into the compound to complete their task. Some minutes later Beth heard a low clunk, and she could just make out the intruder as they locked the gate at the far end of the site. They turned, and walked towards where Beth was hiding. It was a woman. As she neared Beth's position, she pulled her hood away from her face and unzipped her top to reveal a low-cut T-shirt underneath. She took a pair of dangly earrings out of her pocket and threaded them into her ears as she walked. They were the same earrings she had worn when she kissed Freddie in the bus shelter the night before.

As Tracy neared the railway alley, she stopped to slip off her trainers, quickly swapping them for a pair of red party shoes from her bag. She applied a fresh coat of lipstick without using a mirror and disappeared.

Beth waited a few minutes, removed herself from the

weeds and headed back to the house. As she dropped the application form into the letterbox at the far end of the Marshall's road, she grinned in admiration: Tarty Tracy had just, single-handedly, immobilised an entire fleet of Malvanian jeeps. Stupid Freddie really had got himself involved with the wrong girl.

When she washed and got ready for bed that night she felt exhilarated by the thought that a Resistance cell was active in the village. She lay awake for some time, wondering what other plans were afoot: the village, being so close to the M25, was the perfect place to weaken the Malvanian stronghold on London. It took her a long time to get to sleep and, as she finally dozed off, she thought she could hear the dog next door barking. Daft mutt, she thought, sliding into a dreamy state – it's probably been startled by its own shadow.

She came to a little later - although how much later she couldn't tell - and thought she heard a noise on the landing. Just the house creaking, she thought, and her mind drifted into memories of standing in Melissa's kitchen on the night she set out on her journey.

'Yeah - just the house creaking,' she heard Melissa say.

She became vaguely aware of a third noise, this time very close indeed, but was unable to wake herself up. She turned over and pulled the bedclothes around her ears.

A deluge of light filled the room, penetrating the thin skin of her eyelids and bringing her to her senses. She opened her eyes and instantly recoiled, covering her face with her hands and peering through her fingers.

'Put your hands above your head, right now,' said a voice.

Beth obeyed.

'Tell me who you are and what you are doing in this house.'

Tarty Tracy was standing at the bottom of the bed, and she was pointing a P229 pistol at Beth's forehead.

Chapter Twenty-Three
Confrontation

'Snap,' said Beth.

She had pulled her gun from under the pillow and was aiming it at Tracy's chest.

Tracy's face twitched. 'Where did you get that?'

'Same source as you.'

'You don't look old enough.'

'I'm not.'

'If I were to pull this trigger, I'd be shooting a child. Correct?'

'Correct.'

'If I put my gun down will you shoot me?'

'No.'

'I don't trust you.'

'If I was a Malvanian collaborator I would have killed you in the jeep enclosure.'

Tracy nodded. Without taking her eyes off Beth, she reached to one side, placed her pistol on Lucy's dressing table and stepped away. Beth threw her gun onto the rug beside the bed and sat up. She could feel her Swiss army knife pressing into her thigh: it would take a split second to retrieve it if she needed it.

Tracy's right hand flexed involuntarily. Beth could

see the outline of a similar knife in the pocket of Tracy's jeans, just centimetres from her immaculately nail-varnished fingers.

'How long have you been here?' she said.

'Two nights.'

'How did you get into the village?'

'I walked in when you were snogging Fart-Head Freddie in the bus shelter. You were late that night. I thought you weren't coming.'

'You noticed that?'

'Of course. I'm Beth, by the way. I thought what you did tonight was brilliant.'

'Thank you.' Tracy's right hand relaxed, her fingers no longer zoning in on the knife. 'I'm guessing I don't need to tell you I'm called Tracy.'

She stepped forward and shook Beth's hand. 'I was cacking myself in that enclosure. Didn't have enough sugar in the end so I put a potato up the exhaust pipe of the last one.'

She caught sight of herself in Lucy's mirror and rearranged her movie-star hair. She smiled. 'Fart-Head Freddie. I like it.'

***

Doug Hardy raised his hands to his head in frustration.

'Have you gone ruddy mad, Jane?'

He walked over to Peter's bed and sat down.

'If we report her missing,' he said, 'the Malvanians will do God knows what to her. You know that.'

Jane sank on to the bed beside him. 'Couldn't we

137

pretend she's ill?' she said. 'And say she ran off because she's depressed?'

'And how do we explain why we haven't reported it for nearly a month?' He buried his face in his hands. 'If they find her in London they'll know she's been gone for ages. I don't fancy our chances if they realise we've been lying to them, do you?'

'What if she's been injured? Surely it's better the Malvanians find her than she never comes back at all!'

'We have a son too – or have you forgotten? If they haven't injected him full of yellow crap already they will after this! Or is Beth more important than Peter now?'

They had argued yesterday - and the day before - and Doug knew they would never agree. With her back to him, Jane curled herself into a ball on the bed, clutching Aunty Mu's old mobile phone in both hands. She repeatedly dialled Beth's number, breathing a whimper through her lips every time it went to voicemail.

'For God's sake!' He yelled so loudly that Jane let go of the phone and clutched Peter's duvet instead, as if she were clinging to the side of a treacherous mountain.

'She's had the bloody thing turned off for weeks, Jane! She's not going to answer it!'

He stood up and looked at her, breathing heavily; too angry to comfort her, and unable to find the words to apologise.

'I'll make a pot of coffee,' he muttered, and walked out of the room.

***

Next door, Harold Stone was lurking in his study, pressing the rim of a drinking glass against the wall that adjoined Peter's bedroom. The other end of the glass was wedged against his ear. His eyes widened, he reached for his notebook and wrote what he had just heard in a hasty scrawl. Then he skulked over to the computer. He drummed his fingernails on the desk as he waited for the website of the Malvanian People's Party to load, and followed the links to the *KONTAKT* section. He adjusted his spectacles, and typed with such relish that a string of saliva fell from his half-open mouth like elastic, before dripping onto the computer keyboard and disappearing between the keys.

Chapter Twenty-Four
Sisters in Arms

Beth handed Tracy a second mug of coffee.

'Thanks,' she said, taking a mouthful and leaving a bright red lipstick mark on the rim. 'I can't believe you've got this far by yourself.'

Beth had told her about everything – except Ricky. There was no way she could admit she had run away from the Resistance bunker because of him. It made her look immature.

'Are you and Freddie for real?' she asked.

Tracy grimaced. 'No. It's my job to create an access point in and out of the village. Same time, same place every night.'

'Isn't that a bit weird? Having to ...'

'Have a relationship with someone you can't stand? It's horrible. But worth it - all sorts of people and equipment have got through the gap I create: weapons and ammunition, 'clean' mobile phones – quite a few British Army personnel too. Some are hiding in the village, some move on again after a couple of days.'

'What happens if you can't make it one night, or another soldier gets put on patrol?'

'We have a signal. I go and visit Mrs Gibbs who lives

in the house opposite the access point. She's in her eighties so it's plausible that I'd call in occasionally. I let her know there's a problem, and later on in the day, she puts a note out for the milkman, rolled up and stuck in a milk bottle. Anyone planning to come in or out that night will see the note and know it's not safe.'

Mrs Gibbs sounded great. Beth wanted to ask Tracy what happened to all the extra milk that got delivered, but decided against it. She was determined to look grown-up.

'Why did you choose Freddie?'

'I've been trained to pick people the Resistance can use. The soldiers all drink in a pub near the railway station. If you hang around long enough, watching body language and catching bits of conversation, you start to see people's weak spots: maybe they've got a grudge against their boss, or secretly they're not happy about being here. Maybe they like money a bit too much …'

'So you can bribe them?'

'We blackmail them too. One of the soldiers was always talking about his sick kid, so someone in the village bought him a few drinks and said he would pay him for electrical goods. The soldier stole a laptop from the Malvanian army, and sold it so he could send money back home. Unfortunately the transaction was filmed. He'd be shot if his commanding officer saw the video, so he does whatever we tell him. He was the soldier on guard duty in the jeep compound tonight. He just sat with his back to the window and turned the radio up.'

'Are you blackmailing Freddie?'

'Nothing so complicated. You watch them at work,

too, and see if anyone has a sloppy attitude. Freddie stood out from the start: smoking cigarettes when he should be concentrating; not looking at people's papers properly. And he made it obvious that he was looking for a British girlfriend. He was an easy target.'

She looked at her watch. 'I should go before it gets light. It's been really good to meet you, you know?' She gave Beth a hug. 'I've enjoyed having someone to talk to – I can't talk to my own family.'

'Why don't you come round again? Tomorrow? We could …'

'No.' Tracy examined her nails. 'I came here tonight to find out who you are. Now I know. If I visit again I will be drawing attention to you. And, more importantly, you could draw attention to us.' She adjusted her shoulder bag. 'My advice to you is to get out of here as quickly as possible and leave us to do our work unhindered. Good luck Beth.'

She opened the kitchen door and left without looking back.

That hurt. Beth felt as if she was six years old and nobody wanted to play with her. Why did everyone make her feel like a kid all the time? The fridge hummed noisily in the silence, and she felt angry that she was alone again. Julie had warned her that resistance work was lonely - but it ruddy well wasn't fair. Her heart burned inside her: she had never hated her life as much as she did right now. She picked up Tracy's mug, threw the leftover coffee into the sink and washed up, crabbily removing Tracy's lipstick mark with a dishcloth.

She ran upstairs and dived into bed. The duvet

cocooned her, but it was not enough. All she wanted was a cuddle from her mum. I never want to get out of bed again, she thought. As the dawn broke, she cried herself into a deep and self-protecting sleep.

She woke at two o'clock in the afternoon. The imprints of Tracy's high heels were still on the rug, and as Beth looked at them she felt her hand move instinctively towards her knife again. She took it out from under the pillow and examined it. Her fingers itched to use it, and she flicked out the various blades in turn, watching them catch and reflect the light seeping in round the edge of the curtains.

She managed to raise half a smile as she remembered how useless she'd been at describing the knife during her first observation and memory test at the bunker. Forsyth's face was a picture when she said the screwdriver-bottle-opener was 'a blunt knife with a lump taken out'. She hadn't even noticed the little notch lower down which was for stripping and preparing electric wires.

She sat up and Forsyth's words returned to her: 'We have to be the best we can, no matter how bad we feel.' He was right, of course, and she got up and dressed, switching on Lucy's computer before going downstairs to make herself breakfast. Then, with a mug of coffee in one hand, a bowl of tinned fruit in the other and a marmite-on-toast sandwich between her teeth, she went back up to the bedroom and surfed the internet to try and find out more about the Malvanians. Every now and then, a noise outside would catch her curiosity, and she looked through a gap in the curtains and watched the street. What Tracy had said about spotting people's weaknesses was very interesting, and Beth tried to analyse the characters of the men and women who were walking by.

She resolved to do as much research as she could over the next few days whilst she waited to hear about her Youth Camp placement. To keep her fitness levels high, she would exercise for one hour a day. She would re-read everything she had found out about the Marshalls and search the house again for more information. She must watch Malvanian television programmes and keep learning the language.

She had a feeling the next few days were going to fly by.

***

The letterbox squeaked open and clunked shut. It had been seventy-two hours since she had posted the application form. She walked into the hallway and picked up the envelope that was lying on the doormat. It was addressed to Lucy, and it was sealed with the logo of the Malvanian People's Party.

She glared at the little picture of the sword-wielding eagle with the globe in its claws, and ripped open the envelope. Inside was a travel pass, a photo ID card and the Malvanian Youth Handbook. A letter thanked her for her application, and gave her details of her journey.

Her heart racing, she scanned the letter to see if she had been sent to Peter's camp. *Please* let it be South East London, she thought.

She kicked the wall in frustration, and paced up and down the hallway, trying to think fast.

Was it possible that she could use the skills that Tracy had told her about? Could she find a 'mark', a person whom she could manipulate to get her into Peter's camp?

The letter said she would 'make lots of new chums'. What if she could make friends with someone who could help her rescue her brother?

According to her travel pass, she was to leave for London in three hours. She had already packed Lucy's suitcase with everything she needed, and there was nothing else to do but wait until it was time to leave.

She could hardly bear it.

Chapter Twenty-Five
Parallel Motion

Beth sat on the London-bound train watching the world slide by.

She leant drowsily against the glass and half-watched as the green-and-beige mosaic of houses and gardens thinned out and became the rolling emeralds, sages and olives of the green belt. The train plunged into a wood, and she could just make out a battery of Malvanian artillery guns through the trees, manned by hard-faced soldiers and surrounded by camouflage nets and barbed wire. The train entered a tunnel carved into the side of a hill, and Beth looked at her reflection in the darkened window: sometimes clear, sometimes near-obliterated by the flashes of light created by maintenance lamps attached to the tunnel wall. She started to doze off, idly counting the lights as the train chugged forwards … thirty-six, thirty-seven, thirty-eight … … fifty-one, fifty-two …

Her ears popped as the train burst out from the other side of the hill and the air pressure dropped. Bright sunlight flooded into the carriage, and the surrounding fields seemed to white-out for a moment or two. Her eyes re-adjusted to the light, and what she saw banished her sleepiness and made her shiver.

The verdant grass of the English countryside had been violated by a fleet of a thousand - maybe two thousand - Malvanian tanks. They stood in three rows, stretching in both directions as far as the eye could see. Two rows pointed outwards to defend the capital city of Britain from its own people, and the massive guns of the inner row faced towards London, daring anyone to try and escape. They had been painted to blend in with their surroundings, but the cold, inorganic metal conflicted with the living landscape, and the two would never be one. The Malvanians had carved up the grass, flattened fences and demolished hedgerows. In the distance, a half-ruined church smouldered from a recent Malvanian attack. Imposing metal lookout towers stood tall amongst the tanks, search equipment and guns swivelling from the turrets at the top.

The train hurtled past. Signs at the trackside warned the drivers to keep to the maximum speed, and an announcement on the train told the passengers to stay in their seats, not to take photographs, and not to attempt any action that might be considered a threat to Malvanian authority. The snipers in the towers nearest the railway line levelled their guns on the carriage windows as the train passed, and the surveillance cameras traced every movement in a slow, predatory arc.

The doors at the end of the carriage swished open and an armed guard asked to see everyone's tickets. She had the reddest hair Beth had ever seen, swept glamorously under her Malvanian railway worker's hat.

She smelled of violets - but the bullets in the steel-grey sub-machine gun strapped to her chest were capable of slicing a human being in half. She thanked everyone as they showed their tickets, then disappeared into the next carriage with another swish.

The suburbs of London were soon in sight. Beth could see checkpoints stationed at every block; groups of soldiers flagging down vehicles at gunpoint, checking under cars with mirrors and opening up vans and lorries. Lone armoured trucks patrolled the streets at intervals, and the *Komplianz* squads prowled, looking for their next victim. Beth leant back in her seat, logging everything that she saw and cross-referencing it with the briefings at the Resistance bunker.

The train descended into another tunnel, the lights started flashing hypnotically, and Beth felt the drowsiness return, creeping up on her like a fog. Before she had counted up to twenty, she had fallen asleep.

***

Harold Stone drove into London in his old brown car with the dent in the side where it had been hit by a motorbike.

He turned onto a wide, suburban A-road and hummed to himself as the early morning sun warmed him through the car window. To his right was a golf course; to his left, a railway line. A train travelling towards London caught up with the car, and for a short while the two vehicles ran in tandem. Harold glanced sideways at the train. He was level with the guard's cab, and couldn't help noticing that the guard was a young lady with the most extraordinary red hair, swept up -

like an air hostess - under a jaunty little cap. He smirked and hummed more loudly. He had always been partial to a redhead.

The train lurched forward and began to leave the car behind. Harold took a final look at the pretty train guard, and the car swerved slightly, causing another motorist to beep their horn at him. Regaining his concentration, he hunched himself over the steering wheel and fixed his eyes on the road ahead.

On the passenger seat beside him was a brown paper bag. Phyllis had given him a packed lunch with his favourite muffins, but he wasn't hungry. The excitement of meeting the Malvanian Chief of Informants had taken his appetite away.

Chapter Twenty-Six
People to Meet

'*Prezenten dennen Identitie-Kard.*'

The soldier guarding the entrance to Youth Camp 476 inhaled noisily. He checked Beth's details, unaware that she was observing him.

She could see the reflection of the sky in his boots, and his nails were manicured to perfection. His posture said 'I would rather die than slouch', and his chest bore the ribbon of the *Qualitätz-Gefolgen-Laurel:* the Malvanian Medal for Loyal Service.

'*Dennen passen.* You may pass.' He was no Freddie. His eyes were cold, and Beth knew that he would never help her in a million years.

She walked through the main entrance and approached the desk, where a small woman sat.

'Good afternoon!'

The woman checked the clock behind her: it was one minute to twelve.

'It is still ze morning,' she said, without any hint of humour.

Her name badge said '*Rezeptioniszt: Brenda Klumm*'. Her hair was immaculate; her desk impossibly tidy. Already, Beth knew that Brenda was too inflexible to be a 'mark'.

Brenda swiped Beth's ID card and handed it back.

'Thank you, Lucy Marshall.'

She tapped out a single, shrill note on a bell on the desk.

After a lengthy wait, a much younger, ginger-haired woman appeared from an adjoining room, and Brenda rebuked her for taking too long. According to her badge, this young woman was '*Sub-Klerk: Anna Schmitt*'. She handed Beth a transparent plastic *Skoolpak*.

'I am sorry for the delay,' said Anna. She looked sad. 'Here is your writing and drawing equipment, your Malvanian Youth Promise - written in English and Malvanian - and your Malvanian dictionary.'

'Thanks,' said Beth. Anna's low position and unhappy demeanour made her potentially useful, and Beth really wanted to talk to her. But Anna returned to her room, and Brenda clicked her tongue in annoyance.

A short while later a third woman appeared.

'This is ze Matron, Berta Sedlak,' said Brenda. 'Matron means 'mother' - therefore she is your new mother whilst you are away from home.'

Beth studied the new arrival's hairy nostrils and big, sausage fingers. She wasn't sure Matron was even a woman, let alone anybody's mum.

'Follow me,' said Matron, and led Beth down the corridor. 'Always walk on the right,' she said. 'And no talking.'

She took Beth up three flights of stairs to a brightly lit landing, where she turned and spoke.

'Here are ze dormitories.'

'Thank you. Can I ask - what if I need someone in the night?'

'Vot do you mean?'

'If I get upset in the night. You being my new mum and all that.'

'You vill not be upset. Being at camp is a happy time. If your *stomach* gets upset, then zat is different. You can go to the medical room and get a tablet.'

Berta had no maternal instincts. She could not be manipulated.

'Lights out is at nine thirty p.m.; wake up call is at six a.m.; bathroom usage is on a rota - check the sheet in your dormitory - take ten minutes only to wash and dress, please. Breakfast is at half past seven. You may talk only in ze bedrooms and ze dining room. Now. Go to your dormitory and get changed into your new uniform.'

The navy blue uniform was laid out on her bed, and Beth put it on. She returned to the corridor, where Berta was waiting for her.

'I vill escort you to your first class,' she said.

They returned to the ground floor, crossed a courtyard and entered another building.

'Citizenship is for all ages,' said the Matron. 'After that you vill follow ze girls of your own age to your maths lesson.' She knocked on a door and opened it.

The Citizenship teacher smiled from the front of the classroom and pointed to a couple of empty seats.

'Sit where you like, make yourself at home and join in when you can.' She turned to her interactive whiteboard and touched the screen.

Citizenship module 10

The secret of how to be a girl:
Know your place and do as you are told.

'Vem starten talken?' asked the teacher. *'Vat issen zee lowlisch -spöt vom damsels in zee societie Malvanisch?'*

There was an empty chair next to the window, and Beth sat down beside a girl with mousy hair.

'Welcome!' whispered the girl. 'My name's Trudy.'

'Vem hatten koncept?' asked the teacher. *'Vem talken?'*

'Isn't this fantastic?' whispered Trudy. She put her hand up, smiled proudly and answered the question in fluent Malvanian.

Chapter Twenty-Seven
On a Mission

Harold Stone drove across Westminster Bridge and parked in Parliament Square.

Where Big Ben had once overlooked the Thames, a shiny metal tower now stood, crowned with a steel and glass digital clock. As he crossed the street, two doors underneath the clock silently opened. A mechanical eagle slid out and announced that it was fourteen hundred hours, Central Malvanian Time. On the opposite side of the road, a giant photograph of Smit the clown chuckled from a billboard:

KLOWNEN LAFFEN OOR SCOURGEN
Laugh With Me Or Be Punished.

He walked up the steps to the Ministry of Informants, showed his papers to the soldier on guard duty and was ushered inside.

'Good morning, Mr Stone,' said the man at the reception desk.

'We have - as I believe they say in ze films - been expecting you.' He smiled broadly at his own joke.

Harold's face broke into a grin that exposed his crooked teeth. He was enjoying his little trip to London enormously.

'Please wait here, my friend,' said the receptionist, gesturing to Harold to sit on a sofa in the corner.

'Thank you,' he replied. He sank back into the cushions, running his fingers over the upholstery. He breathed in the aroma of the room: a mixture of floor polish and freshly brewing coffee. It was the most alluring smell he had ever encountered.

A senior officer in the Malvanian Army approached him, his hand outstretched in welcome. Harold jumped to his feet and, in the excitement of the moment, saluted.

The Officer laughed. 'Good day, sir,' he said. 'I am most happy to meet you. Let us enjoy some fine coffee together, and then you can share ze information you have brought.'

Harold parted his lips in order to speak, but no words would come out. A gurgle of satisfaction purred in his throat, and he followed the Malvanian into his office.

***

'Excuse me,'

It was the end of the Citizenship lesson, and the teacher looked up from her desk.

'I'm sorry to bother you,' said Beth, 'but my ruler and protractor seem to be missing from my *Skoolpak*.'

This wasn't true. She had wrapped them in her handkerchief and hidden them behind a radiator.

'*Miz remorzlich* - I am very sorry,' said the teacher. 'You must go and get a replacement. Hurry now.'

Brenda frowned when Beth arrived back in the reception area.

'Zis is not acceptable,' she said, and struck the desk bell with force.

The door at the back opened and - as Beth had hoped - Anna reappeared.

'*Vot iszt dis?*' Brenda tipped the contents of the *Skoolpak* onto the counter, and Anna hung her head.

'*Sorten dee immediatzlich,*' said Brenda. '*Is dee dumm? Is dee imbecile?*'

The phone rang, and Brenda answered it. Beth caught Anna's eye and smiled sympathetically.

'*Miz remorzlich.*'

'*Zanken zee.*' Anna seemed touched.

Brenda cupped her hand round the telephone mouthpiece and glared. '*Dinnen talken! Sorten dee!*'

Crimson with embarrassment, Anna walked to the store cupboard and returned with the 'missing' items.

'*Zanke,*' said Beth. '*Zanke, Damsel Schmitt.*'

'Call me Anna - please,' Anna whispered, and she hurried away into the office at the rear. As she did so, Brenda finished her phone call and spat more insults after her.

'*Dummskull ... Klansicker!*'

'Er, where do I go for maths?' asked Beth.

'Room C12,' said Brenda. 'Down ze corridor and turn right, then follow ze signs to C Block.'

'Thanks,' said Beth.

At the end of the corridor she stopped and pretended to tie her shoelace. She glanced behind her: Brenda was busy on the phone. Instead of turning right, she headed left into the heart of the administration block, and began a reconnaissance sweep of the offices on the ground floor:

- Room one: *Photokopy & Media* - at least two photocopiers and a laminator. Door locked - a sign says that Brenda has the key.
- Room two: *Rekord & Arkive*. Shelves and shelves of papers. Name on door: *Arkivist: Humfrey Klacker* - sweet-looking old man, but his body language says ex-military - his top drawer has a padlock: does he keep a gun in it?
- Room three: *Kurrikulum* - miserable woman with hair in a bun is talking on the telephone. Door badge says '*Olga Binnz … Skool izt Funn.*'
- Room four: Stationery cupboard. Can't see in - Brenda has the key.

Room five was the Chief Administrator's office. As Beth approached, the door opened and the caretaker came out.

'I'll sort it now, Patti,' he said.

He walked away, leaving a strong smell of body odour lingering in the air. Through a gap in the door, Beth watched the Chief Administrator pick up a can of air freshener and spray it round the room. A whiff of lavender disinfectant seeped into the corridor.

- So, room five: Chief Administrator: *Patti Novak* - has three pairs of spectacles and doesn't like bad smells.
- There is a fire extinguisher bolted to the wall by room five.

- Room six: *Sub-Klerk: Valda Goög* - she is the only person to notice me walking by - she has an exercise bike in the corner of her office.
- Room seven: Ladies' toilets.
- Room eight: Caretaker's den. Instead of 'sorting out' the Chief Administrator's problem, he has sat down to have a long cup of coffee and a biscuit. He, too, sees me - but he doesn't care. He is English.

She returned to the main corridor. Brenda was re-tidying her desk and did not notice her.

She hurried to C Block and found Room 12. The maths teacher looked annoyed.

'*Sitten immediatzlich!*'

Beth smiled innocently.

'Sorry I'm late,' she lied. 'I'm new and I got lost.'

***

That night she sat on her bed, thumbing through the pages of her Malvanian dictionary. When Brenda had called Anna a '*Dummskull*' it had been easy to guess what it meant. But '*Klansicker*' wasn't so obvious. She searched for the definition.

Klansicker n (*derogatory*) a homesick person; someone whose focus - or dedication to a cause - is compromised because their thoughts are elsewhere. An airhead; (*inf*) a loser.

Perfect, thought Beth. She would definitely use Anna to get herself a transfer to Peter's camp.

There was a jolt as somebody sat on her bed uninvited.

'Hi, Lucy.'

It was Trudy, the girl she had sat next to in Citizenship class. Beth forced a smile.

'Glad to see you're working on speaking the language,' said Trudy. '*Wid Malvanische-talken kommet Bennifitz:* with the Malvanian language comes privilege.'

Beth couldn't be bothered to reply; she was busy planning the lies she was going to tell Anna.

'Of course. You want to study,' said Trudy. 'I commend you, sister.'

Trudy left her alone, and Beth kept her head buried in her new, 'favourite' book. After half an hour a bell sounded, and she got into bed. A short time afterwards the lights went out. She dropped the dictionary quietly onto the floor, its pages already curled at the edges, where the sweat from her fingers had seeped into the paper.

Her eyes wide open, she continued to plan and think.

The sooner she could leave this awful place the better.

Chapter Twenty-Eight
Missing You

Peter lay in his bed in the dark, hardly daring to move. The worst thing had happened. The science teacher had told Daniel off for getting his circuit board wrong, and Daniel had burst out crying and shouted that he hated the teacher, he hated science and he wanted his mummy.

And the nurse had come and given him an injection.

Daniel had collapsed to the ground, his back arched like a scorpion - and then a little bit of sick had come out of his mouth. Because of this, the nurse had taken him away for 'observation' - but now he was in bed, asleep.

Every now and then Daniel snored - and Peter felt scared. His Grandpa had died in the night from something called a 'stroke', and Nana had said that he was snoring (which was something he never usually did) and the doctor said afterwards that snoring was a sign of having a stroke. And Nana said IF ONLY SHE'D KNOWN THAT BEFOREHAND she could have woken Grandpa up and called an ambulance before it was too late.

And also, Justin Baldwin said that people can die if they're sick in their sleep, because it goes into their lungs and they can't breathe and they drown in their own puke.

The whole day had been horrible. Some of the children had been told they were going home. A teacher came and read out a list of all the 'lucky' children, but Peter's name wasn't on it. He stood like a statue whilst his friends jumped and whooped with excitement around him. Then he was summoned to the Headteacher's office for something called an 'appraisal'.

'You are a very good boy,' said the Headteacher. 'But we are anxious that you are not learning to speak Malvanian quickly enough.'

It was true: he found Malvanian words really difficult and he was always getting them muddled up.

'It is important that you take our language home with you when you leave,' continued the Headteacher. 'Your family must see that you are a good Malvanian citizen.'

He picked up a book from his desk and gave it to Peter.

'Here is something to help you learn quickly. I am sure that, if you work a little harder, you will be able to go home very soon.'

As soon as the Headmaster's door closed behind him, Peter ran to the toilets and locked himself in.

Maybe if he learnt the whole book right now, he could go back to the Headteacher and show him how clever he was and the Headteacher would put him on the list after all.

He opened the first page:

Id um gudden. Id um Malvanisch.

He swung his legs happily; he already knew those off by heart.

Id um Kompliantliszch
I am obedient

Id um Komplitliszch
I am fully converted

He shut the book and tried to repeat them back to himself, but already the two words beginning with 'K' were getting mixed up in his brain. He screwed his eyes shut and tried to concentrate harder, but it only got more muddled.

He gave up and turned to another page:

Mennen Momma ind Papa nochts allen kennen
My mother and father do not know everything

Mennen Momma ind Papa nochts anlen Kinnen
My mother and father are no longer my main family

This was even more difficult to remember. Repeatedly, he looked at the page, closed the book and tried to make himself learn. But the harder he tried, the more confusing the words became. His head started to hurt and he bent the book in half between his hands. There was a photograph of a little boy on the front cover, and he was reading a Malvanian newspaper that bore the headline:

ALLEN GUDDEN YUZE SPECHEN
ÜBERGLÜBENTUNGEN
All good children speak the best language in the world

Peter clenched his hand into a fist and punched the little boy in the face. He threw the book on the floor and cried until he ran out of tears and his tummy hurt.

Back in the dormitory in the dark, Daniel made a spluttering noise and Peter's heart leapt. Holding his own breath so that he could hear more clearly, he waited anxiously for his friend to exhale. Finally the out-breath came, and Peter sighed with relief.

Please God - don't let Daniel die.

I don't want to be on my own.

He sucked his thumb and twiddled his fringe around his finger.

And please God, can Beth come and take me home tomorrow?

Chapter Twenty-Nine
Manipulation

Beth and Trudy were walking along the second floor corridor of the Humanities block.

From the other direction, Anna came down the corridor towards them carrying a pile of books. As Anna passed them, Beth faked a stumble and collided with Anna, nudging her hard. The books fell to the floor.

'Oh, I'm so sorry,' said Beth, stooping immediately to pick them up.

'It is my fault,' said Anna. She rubbed her arm where Beth had struck her and looked forlornly at the scattered books.

'I'll help,' said Trudy, kneeling down to pick up a Geography textbook.

'No,' said Beth. 'You go ahead. This is the perfect opportunity for me to practice speaking Malvanian, right?'

Trudy nodded, and waited until everyone had gone into the History room. 'Your commitment to learn the language is impressive,' she whispered. 'I'll explain to the teacher why you're late.'

When Trudy had gone, Beth collected the books and gave them back to Anna, and Anna burst into tears.

'Please leave!' she said. 'You vill be punished!'

'I won't,' said Beth, and she touched Anna on the arm. 'Please don't cry.' She remembered that nobody was in the Geography room when they walked past. 'Would you like to sit down for a while? Until you feel better.'

Anna nodded, and Beth guided her to the empty classroom. Anna pulled out a chair and sat down. Beth handed her a tissue.

'*Zanke*,' said Anna, blowing her nose. 'You know, I hate zis place.'

'They're lucky to have you,' said Beth.

'Brenda doesn't think so. She is ze worst woman. I hate her.'

Anna inspected the tissue, looking for a dry area to wipe her eyes with. 'She has no soul.'

Beth gave her a clean hanky.

'You are very kind,' said Anna.

'If you don't mind me saying so, you seem very young to be working abroad,' said Beth.

'I am just nineteen.'

'You must miss your family.'

Anna shrugged. 'My mother and father not so much - but I miss my little brother. He is called Max and he is four years old.'

She dipped her fingers into the gap between her collar and her neck, pulled out a silver locket on a chain and opened it. A beautiful child with curls of auburn hair smiled from a tiny photo.

'When did you last see him?'

'Nearly three months. It is too long. Brenda says I am a fool for being so...' She searched for the English word.

165

'Attached?' She gazed at Max's picture. 'But whenever I open this, it is as if ze sun shines especially for me.'

Beth could not reply at first. A torrent of emotion rose inside her and - for a moment - she was tempted to tell Anna that, she too, was a devoted older sister. But the lies and manipulation had to continue. She drew on every last muscle and nerve fibre and steadied her voice.

'I know how you feel. I am an only child, but I have a little cousin - Peter. He is the nearest thing I have to a brother, and I love him dearly. He is at a different camp to me...' Now, the lies became the truth: 'He is seven years old. Not as young as Max, but too young to be...' Her voice cracked. 'Too young to be without any of his family.'

She cried real tears, but she felt ill at ease with herself. She knew she was using her sadness to get what she wanted. Feeling dirty, she allowed Anna to put her arms around her and hold her. Anna, too, began to cry again.

The moment had come.

'Could you help me?' Beth's heart raced with a mixture of guilt and expectation. 'Will you arrange for me to move to Peter's camp?'

'I am not sure...'

'I just need the correct papers.'

Anna shifted uncomfortably.

'Of course, that's fine. Forget it. You don't want to upset Brenda.' Beth brushed a tear from her eye and stood up to leave. 'I understand. You mustn't break the rules.'

She turned her back on Anna and walked to the door.

'No - wait!'

When Beth turned, there was a fire burning in Anna's

eyes. She kissed the locket emphatically and returned it to the safety of her chest.

'I *will* break ze rules.' Her fists were clenched. 'If Brenda gets upset… well, good. It will bring some warmth to her cold, dead heart. It will give me joy to reunite you with your dear cousin. Yes - I will do it for lonely children everywhere.'

Beth flopped back down into the chair. She'd done it - but it did not feel good.

'Who authorises the transfers?'

'The Chief Administrator, Patti Novak. But you will never get into her office. She is inside all day, even for her lunch. If she goes out - even for a minute - she locks the door. She is ze last to leave at night - and then ze security alarm is switched on. It is impossible.'

'Does anyone else have a key to Patti's office?'

'Brenda has ze master key.'

'Could you steal it for me?'

'Yes.' Anna seemed revitalised.

'I have to go to my class. Can you come back here tonight?'

Anna nodded, her flame-red hair glowing in the morning light.

'Tell me what I need to do, Lucy, and I will do it.'

Chapter Thirty
Things Unseen

Beth scooped a large handful of prawns from her lunch plate and dropped them into a plastic bag on her lap. She put the bag in her pocket.

She got up, walked out of the dining hall and made her way to the reception area. Brenda was on her lunch break, and Anna was at the desk. Beth cast a glance at Anna, and indicated with her hand that Anna should wait five minutes before carrying out her part of the plan. They both checked their watches, and Beth walked into the administration block.

She went past Valda Goög's office: Valda, too, was having lunch, sitting on her exercise bike with her back to the door, a diet drink in one hand and a brown rice cake in the other. Beth ducked into the ladies' toilet. She took out the bag of prawns, emptied half of them into a sock and pressed them behind the hot water heater. She turned the thermostat to 'High'.

She waited. Five minutes had now passed - and Anna would be on the phone to Patti Novak, telling her she was needed urgently at the reception desk. After a while she heard a door open and close again, and footsteps hurry into the distance. She slipped out of the toilets and walked swiftly towards Patti's office. The room was empty, and locked. Beth looked up and down the corridor, then slid her hand behind the fire extinguisher. Attached with Blu-tack to the underside of the wall bracket was Brenda's master key. Anna had done it!

Beth let herself into Patti's office and locked the door behind her. She opened the window as wide as it would go and sprayed out the contents of the air freshener until it was empty, returned the window to its original position and put the freshener back on the desk. She took out the remaining prawns and, one by one, poked them into the hem of the office curtains, easing them between the stitches with a pencil. The office was south facing, and the curtains were warm from the heat of the sun.

Her job completed, Beth left the office. She returned the master key to its hiding place behind the fire extinguisher, skulked out of the admin block and made her way to the Study Room to do her 'Loyalty' homework.

***

Four days later, Beth walked to the dining hall for breakfast. Anna was standing by a notice-board at the end of the corridor, rearranging some posters. When Beth walked by, Anna whispered:

'It has happened!'

Beth walked a few metres round the corner, pretended that she had forgotten something and turned back the way that she had come. By the time she reached the notice-board Anna had already hurried away.

She walked to the administration block. Even before

she reached the main corridor she could hear Patti Novak in the reception area, screaming down the phone to the caretaker:

'*Dis iszt übernastig!* This is intolerable!'

There was a long pause. Beth could imagine the excuses the caretaker was making.

'I will not work in such *befoulen* - such *bestinken* circumstances!'

There was another, shorter pause before Patti interrupted furiously.

'*Dis - iszt - insufferzlig!*'

Beth turned the corner in time to see Patti slam down the phone and shout at Anna instead.

'*Wär iszt Brenda? Id demanden Brenda!*' Her face was almost purple with fury, and she was far too worked up to notice Beth slipping past.

Beth heard Anna say that Brenda was organising a temporary office for Patti on the top floor of the arts block. Patti screamed something about never wanting to sit in her old office again, and Beth walked into the admin department with the intention of retrieving the key to Patti's office from behind the fire extinguisher. But Valda Goög was walking along the corridor towards her. Valda stopped, raised an eyebrow and asked Beth what she was doing.

Beth clutched her stomach, muttered something about period pains and ran towards the toilets. Valda let her pass, but Beth was sure she could feel Malvanian eyes scrutinising her. Not daring to look back, she raced though the toilet door, pushing it so hard with both hands that it flew open and banged against the wall inside. She bent over to get her breath back then stood up again.

Her heart went into suspended animation inside her chest: the caretaker was standing by the sinks, staring at her.

'You again,' he said. He scratched his armpits. 'You are definitely up to no good, young lady.'

Several heartbeats tumbled out at once as her heart tried to regain its rhythm.

'Seen you around here a few times, haven't I?'

The caretaker's itch seemed to spread downwards to his belly, and he rubbed himself vigorously. Beth maintained a poker face.

'Not that I care,' he said. He took a spanner from his tool belt and waved it half-heartedly at a pipe under one of the sinks. 'You can disobey those buggers as much as you like. I hate 'em.'

Beth quietly wiped the nervous sweat from her hands onto the back of her trousers, and breathed a sigh of relief. The caretaker pointed the spanner languidly at another pipe and scratched one of his buttocks.

'Er, if you don't mind,' said Beth. She nodded towards the cubicles.

'Of course, love. Sorry.' He looked embarrassed. 'I could do with a nice, long coffee break anyway,' he said, and shambled back to his den.

As the door bounced shut, Beth decided to remove the prawns from the water heater, as this would keep the caretaker guessing as to the cause of the smell. She pulled out the sock from its hiding place and moved into a cubicle. She gagged as the fetid prawns, and then the sock, fell into the toilet. As soon as she had pulled the flush, she ran to the sink and spat out the vile, fishy taste that had descended from her nose onto her tongue. She washed her hands with several squirts of lemon soap and splashed water on her face to steady her nerves.

She wondered where Valda was. She walked to the door and edged it open until there was a tiny crack, just big enough to see along the corridor towards Patti's office. The coast was clear. She opened the door boldly and walked out, making the slightest of sideways glances towards Valda's room: Valda was nowhere to be seen.

She walked to Patti's office. The door was ajar, and Anna was already inside.

'Guess what?' she said. 'Brenda has asked me to collect some things for Patti - so I am even supposed to be here!' She glowed with excitement. 'Come - I have ze form right here! You can fill it in whilst I find ze correct envelope. Then I can ... how do you say?' She tapped her head to make the English words come. 'I can make a fake of Patti's signature for you!'

Closing the door behind her, Beth sat at Patti's desk whilst Anna disappeared behind a shelving unit in search of the envelope. The form was a single side of A4, and Beth filled in her details quickly.

State your reasons for this transfer:

She was now in buoyant mood, and felt tempted to write 'I hate your stinking guts and I'm coming to steal my brother from right under your fat, knobbly noses'. But instead, she swivelled round on Patti's office chair so that she could call to Anna and ask her the best thing to say.

As she turned her back on the door she heard it open. Footsteps trod the office floor. For a moment she sat completely still, as if this would somehow make her invisible - but her school uniform would have already given her away, and she slowly turned back round: Humfrey Klacker, the old Malvanian archivist had walked into the room.

For several, achingly long moments he said nothing. He stood, bolt upright, fixing her with a strange, steely gaze. His eyes seemed dead, as if he had killed a hundred people and didn't care if he had to kill one more.

'I am very surprised to see you here,' Humfrey said in Malvanian, his eyes remaining motionless and cold.

The inside of Beth's mouth felt sticky and stale, and she swallowed hard, trying to think of an excuse for being in Patti's office.

'*Zee ist grümpisch, Humfrey!*'

Anna appeared from behind the shelves and spoke cheerfully to the archivist in their mother tongue. 'She is in a bad mood! She won't talk to anyone right now!'

'Indeed, the smell is very bad,' said Humfrey.

'I see you have some papers. Let me take them.' Anna stepped forward and Humfrey handed her a document wallet. 'I can take them to Patti's new office. I am sure she is very grateful.'

To Beth's surprise, Humfrey allowed Anna to take him by the arm and escort him to the door. He asked no more questions, nor gave Beth a second look. Anna closed the door behind him, returned to the desk and gave Beth a brown envelope pre-addressed to the Transfers Office.

'Here it is!' She looked at Beth's transfer form.

'For your reasons for moving, just say 'to further my development as a Malvanian citizen'. It flatters them.'

'Wait a minute! What just happened?'

Anna seemed completely un-flustered by the encounter with Humfrey and smiled.

'Won't he tell someone?' said Beth.

'Don't you know?' said Anna. 'Humfrey is … what is the word? He cannot see anything.'

A laugh of disbelief shot out of Beth's mouth like a cough.

'It is true,' said Anna. 'He is an old soldier who has served in ze army for many years. In my country, such men are rewarded for their loyalty by getting a job for life. Any job. Even if - like Humfrey - they are not able to carry it out.'

Anna picked up Humfrey's document wallet and took out the papers to show Beth. They were mostly blank.

'See?' she said. 'He moves ze papers from one office to ze other, and he thinks he is doing a good job. He is too proud to use his white stick, so he remembers ze number of footsteps to take him around ze building.' She shrugged. 'His country has thanked him, and he is happy.'

'Ruddy hell,' said Beth. She filled in the remainder of the form; Anna forged Patti's signature, put the paper in the envelope and dropped it into Patti's 'Out' tray.

'And now we must go,' said Anna.

There was a noise outside the door, and the handle started to turn.

'Anna? Anna!'

It was Valda.

Chapter Thirty-One
Lies

'Quick!' said Anna. 'Get under the desk!'

Beth dived into the space between the computer's central processing unit and the printer, and Valda walked into the room.

'*Gudden mornen, Anna.*'

'*Hallo, Valda. Dennen gudden?*'

'*Non - id um grümpisch.*'

'*Trülisch?*'

'*Ya.*'

Over the hum of the hard drive, Beth heard the rustle of documents.

'*Rekognizen den Britsich damsel? Hezt namen iszt Lucy Marshall.*'

'*Non, id non rekognizen.*'

'*Id rekon zee iszt Betraitor. Zerpent.*'

'*Non!*'

'*Zie iszt heer … konstantlisch! Heer in den AdminBlok!*'

Valda walked round the desk, pulled up Patti's chair and sat down, crossing her legs. Her left foot was centimetres from Beth's face, and it twitched agitatedly as she continued to talk:

'*Lucy Marshall iszt heer in den mornen - den antenoon - den LünchBreak !*'

Beth winced: Valda had seen her the other day, after all.

'*Dat iszt zuspicious,*' said Valda, and the tip of her shoe brushed against Beth's hair.

Anna quickly moved to Valda's side. She took the computer print-out from Valda and positioned herself between the chair and the shelving unit, so that Valda had to swivel her chair away from Beth if she wanted to see the document.

'*Loöken!*' said Anna. '*Lucy Marshall iszt den FreschStüdent!*'

Valda grunted.

'*Den iszt Fresch ... den iszt Loszt!*' said Anna. '*Den iszt Härmlisch!*'

'*Ya. Loszt. Härmlisch.*'

Valda only sounded half-convinced, but did not say another word about it. Beth became aware that her body was clenched rigid, and allowed herself to relax a little. This released a loud rumble from her breakfast-deprived stomach.

'*Vos iszt dat?*' said Valda, spinning round on the chair.

Beth closed her eyes.

'*WäterPipen!*' said Anna. '*Den stinken - den iszt WäterPipen malfünktion! Ya?*'

Valda stood up.

'*Ya. Den stinken iszt übernastig!*' When she spoke again it sounded as if she had placed her hand over her nose and mouth:

'*Änylich - Id kom heer vor den PoztMail. Vor Patti.*'

Beth heard Anna move over to Patti's 'Out' tray and remove the contents.

'*Zanke,*' said Valda.

Beth heard Valda's shoes move away towards the door. Then she left.

As Beth squeezed herself out from under the desk, Anna was already shredding the computer printout that Valda had left behind.

'Nice of her to post my transfer form for me,' said Beth. She grinned at Anna. 'Well done.'

Anna looked radiant.

'I'd better not come down here again,' said Beth, 'not with snoopy-draws on the prowl.'

Anna held out her hand to Beth.

'It has been such a...privilege to help you,' she said. 'I know I will not see you again, but you will always be my friend.'

An unpleasant mixture of love, triumph and guilt overcame Beth. She let go of Anna's hand and hugged her.

'Thank you for everything,' she said. 'I won't be able to say goodbye when I leave, so I will say it now.'

'*Ya*. Goodbye, dear Lucy.'

'Goodbye, Anna.'

Beth turned and walked away without looking back. It was something she was getting used to.

Chapter Thirty-Two
New Faces

In southeast London, the deep red bricks of the school building glowed like embers in the afternoon sun. Beth rang the entrance bell, and moved her right hand over the wall, feeling its warmth. The door opened.

'Velcome,' said a young woman. 'Come in.'

The woman checked Beth in and told her to leave her suitcase at reception.

'Do you like ze sport?' asked the woman. 'Good! There is ze sport being played right now. I will take you there directly.'

The woman led Beth through several corridors and through a door to the playing field.

'See, vee have all ze sports here,' said the young woman.

In the far corner of the field, one hundred children were doing rhythmic exercises, arranged in ten rows of ten. To the right, a similar number were involved in circuit training, and the rest of the field was being used for games of *Flünken*. Yet it was eerily quiet except for the voices of the Malvanian sports instructors, the whizz of the cannon firing out the *Flünken* discs, and the muffled thud of several hundred pairs of feet treading the grass.

'As you can see, discipline is everything,' said the young woman. 'This is how we learn to be ze best. This way, please.'

The woman led Beth towards one of the *Flünken* matches. As they approached, the children were sent to the side of the playing area for a drinks break. The instructor nodded a greeting to the woman, then beckoned to Beth to approach him. The woman walked away.

'Hello, I'm Lucy.'

'Good day,' he said. 'You know *Flünken*?'

Beth replied that she'd seen it on the television.

'It is ze finest game in the world. And you know why? Because it is fair. Nobody can be ze great vinner or ze show-off. Everybody benefits from *Flünken*. Now you shall meet some of ze other children and learn to play zis wonderful game.'

The two teams returned from their break and gathered around Beth.

'You may speak,' said the instructor. 'Meet your new sister in ze Malvanian Youth.'

A girl of about eighteen stepped forward and said, 'Hi, I'm Sammy.'

Beth was about to introduce herself when a yelp rang out from the back of the group. There was a scuffle, and somebody tried to push to the front. The crowd reluctantly parted and Peter burst out from the ranks. Love and joy were pouring out of his eyes and he was a split second away from jumping up and hugging his beloved sister. The only thing stopping him was his disbelief that this grown-up-looking, blonde girl was really her.

Beth suppressed her desire to scoop Peter up in her arms, and swallowed the wave of painful feeling that was rising in her throat.

'Looks like we have a gatecrasher!' she laughed coolly.

Everybody else laughed too - except Peter, whose face crumpled into an expression of confusion. Beth thought that her heart was going to break into a thousand pieces.

'I'm Lucy Marshall,' she said, and she tried to catch Peter's eye in the hope that he would understand what she was doing. But he was staring at his feet and Beth could see large tears dripping onto the grass.

'I've come from *just outside London* and I need someone to show me around,' she said.

'Ya, Sammy,' said the instructor, 'show Lucy around ze playing field, and explain to her about our wonderful exercise programme and help her to become accustomed to ze wonderful *Flünken!*'

Shooting one last despairing look towards Peter, Beth grabbed hold of Sammy's arm and pulled her away from the group.

'Lead on, sister!' she said.

She walked with Sammy towards the circuit training. A suffocating tightness gripped her chest, and every step she took away from Peter made it worse. Finally she couldn't bear the pain any longer and stopped to look back. He was watching her, his body belittled with rejection. Daniel was at his side, patting him on the head. But Peter was inconsolable. Beth bit her lip and turned her back on him a second time before her own tears could overwhelm her.

Chapter Thirty-Three
Reunion

Beth pushed her supper from one side of her plate to the other. She had not seen Peter since she left the playing field.

'Not hungry?' said Sammy.

'Nah,' said Beth, 'I'm too tired.'

'Come on, I'll show you your dorm,' said Sammy. 'We have to be in bed by nine o'clock anyway.'

They left the dining hall and took a flight of stairs to the second floor. Sammy pointed to a corridor that led off to the left.

'Whatever you do, don't go that way.'

'Why not?' said Beth, peering through the fire doors. 'What's down there?'

'Boys' dorms,' said Sammy. 'Big trouble if you get caught in there. Seriously, the staff are fine if you obey the rules, but if you step out of line you disappear for a week and come back acting really weird.'

She paused, and stared out of the large, arch-shaped window that dominated the landing.

'Electric shock treatment and drugs, I reckon,' she said in a low voice. 'But don't tell anyone – and I mean *anyone* – I said that.'

Beth nodded, and Sammy led her down the corridor on the right. Sammy explained that the dormitories were organised according to age. The room nearest the top of the stairs was for girls aged seven and under. The next was for girls aged eight and nine, the next for ten and eleven year olds, and so on.

'Here we are,' said Sammy. They had arrived at the sleeping quarters for sixteen and seventeen year olds. 'Normally I wouldn't be allowed in, but I am today.'

The dorm was identical to the one at the all-girl camp.

'That's your bed there,' said Sammy.

Beth walked over and sat down on the navy blue bedspread.

'Welcome to Youth Camp 004,' said Sammy. 'Lights out at nine thirty - but I think you'll be fast asleep by then! See you at breakfast tomorrow morning. Sweet dreams, sister!'

Beth hung up her uniform in the cupboard at the side of her bed, unpacked a few items from her rucksack and concealed them in her pockets. She put some pyjamas on over her clothes and got into bed. She ran the layout of the sleeping quarters through her mind. The boys' dormitories would undoubtedly be arranged in the same way as the girls', with the youngest boys sleeping in the dormitory nearest the stairwell. Commander Forsyth had often said that the Malvanians' obsession with rules would be their downfall – and now, their rigid system for organising the bedrooms had saved Beth hours of surveillance. She had already done a recce of the outside of the building when Sammy was showing her the sports activities - and she knew exactly which windows would get her into Peter's dorm later that night.

***

At the Ministry of Informants, Harold Stone was being entertained by his new friends. He laughed loudly at their jokes and admired their shiny uniforms, and they gave him a cigar and toasted him with glasses of expensive wine. He tried to speak Malvanian, and they smiled and gave him more alcohol. He was beginning to feel rather drunk, and through the sweet, alcoholic fug he thought he could see people nudging each other as he slurred and mispronounced his words. But he was having such a wonderful time he didn't care. They even clapped their hands and cheered when he stood on his chair and performed the Malvanian national anthem. When he'd finished singing, he thought he saw someone out of the corner of his eye, putting their fingers in their ears and gesturing that he was a fool. But he was feeling so deliciously numb that he climbed onto the table and began the second verse. Everybody congratulated him on being such a loyal citizen ... and poured more wine into his glass.

***

Under the duvet, Beth listened as thirty-two sixteen and seventeen year-olds filed into the dormitory. Her roommates spoke in low voices, some chatting about the clubs they had attended that evening, and others talking about her and wondering what she would be like. At exactly nine o'clock a bell went and everybody got into bed. A short while later the Matron arrived to check everyone was in their place, and curtly wished them a good night. For the next half hour, some of the girls continued to read or chat; others were quiet. Beth was sure she could hear the girl in the bed next to her crying under the covers. Then another bell rang, and the lights went out. Beth lay on her back in the dark, playing mental arithmetic games to keep herself awake, and after twenty minutes everybody seemed to be asleep. Apart from heavy breathing, all she could hear were the occasional footsteps of the Matron patrolling the corridor.

She got out of bed, slipped off her pyjamas and moved to the open window. She climbed onto the sill and let herself down onto a thin ledge in the wall. To her left was a small horizontal pipe that led to the main drainpipe. It was a metre out of reach and she was ten metres above the ground. Steeling her nerves, she launched herself sideways, letting go of the windowsill with one hand and lunging at the pipe with the other. She felt the force of gravity pulling her body away from the wall and she snatched at the thin tube of metal, floundering and hanging on one-handed, but then her right hand joined her left and brought her body back in contact with the brickwork. She pulled herself along the ledge to the vertical drainpipe. She embraced it and shinned down to the ground.

Keeping close to the school building, she located the big arched window that she had seen when she was on the landing with Sammy; the next four windows along would give her access to the dormitory for boys aged seven and under. There was no drainpipe, but a Virginia creeper had spread its leaves over this side of the school. She grabbed hold of the thickest part of the trunk and began to climb. As she got higher, the branches became thinner and creaked as she searched for hand and footholds - but they held her weight, their hair-like tendrils buried deep in the wall. Two floors up, she slipped through the dormitory window and established herself in a dark corner of the room. She scanned the beds. About halfway down on the right hand side was a figure she recognised. He was curled up on one side, sucking his thumb in his sleep, the other hand clutching a tuft of his blond fringe. Beth rolled along the floor until she reached the bed. There were powdery trails on his cheeks where he had cried himself to sleep. She gently placed one hand over his mouth to prevent him from calling out, and shook his shoulder with the other.

Peter woke and regarded her drowsily. Then he came to his senses and nearly leapt out of bed, emitting a muffled squeal into the palm of her hand.

'Ssshhh!' said Beth.

Peter reached out and touched her blonde hair.

'I knew you'd come,' he said.

Tears splashed down her cheeks. She hugged and kissed him until her knees started aching.

'Listen up,' she said. 'Tomorrow night I'm going to get you out of here.'

Peter's eyes widened. 'And Daniel, too?' he said. 'He

had an injection but he's better now.'

She hesitated. It had not been part of the plan to rescue Daniel - but she could not bring herself to break Peter's heart twice in one day.

'And Daniel, yes. Tomorrow night I will be back to get you. If you see me during the day you must pretend that you don't know me. You must do exactly as I say when I come back. Put your clothes and shoes on underneath your pyjamas but don't let anyone see you. Tell Daniel you are both leaving tomorrow but nothing more. Tell him he has to trust you and that he mustn't tell anyone about it. Have you got that?'

Peter nodded.

'I've got to go now. Go back to sleep. Don't forget: I need you and Daniel to be the best secret keepers in the world, yes?'

She took something out of her pocket.

'See you tomorrow night.'

'Don't go!'

'I have to,' she said. 'Anyway, you won't be alone now. Look!'

She pressed Jackson into Peter's hand.

'It was his idea to come and rescue you. I only came along to keep him company.'

She rolled across the floor, climbed onto the window ledge and disappeared out of sight.

Chapter Thirty-Four
Mission Accomplished

A young Malvanian official called Kurt gripped the seat as the car he was travelling in broke the speed limit through a village just outside the M25. It was four o'clock in the morning.

He pulled down the sun visor to reveal a small mirror and adjusted his hat. He had white blond hair and invisible eyebrows. As he straightened his collar, a van in front of the car suddenly swerved and screeched to a halt outside a large, detached house. The side door slid open, and half a dozen Malvanian soldiers spilled onto the street. They kicked open the gate at the front of the house, ran to the door and forced it open.

The car stopped sharply behind the van. Through one of the downstairs windows of the house, Kurt could see a soldier pushing furniture out of the way, flinging open cupboard doors and ripping down the curtains. He disappeared from sight, and Kurt knew the soldiers would be fanning out into the upstairs rooms, tearing off bedclothes and thrusting their guns into the wardrobes and under the beds.

As he got out of the car, he heard cries of '*Allen id emptisch!*'

This was disappointing, he thought, but he consoled himself with the knowledge that the soldiers were leaving a trail of destruction behind them.

Kurt was part of a team of four - three men and one woman. As the soldiers reappeared and began a search of the gardens, he and his colleagues approached the house. They walked up the path, snapping surgical gloves over their hands, and his female associate issued everyone with polythene specimen bags.

A big dog started barking at the soldiers from the adjoining back garden, hurling itself repeatedly against the fence. Kurt heard a gunshot - and the dog was silenced. A scream rang out from the house next door, but nobody came outside. Kurt walked unemotionally into the hallway and, just as the soldiers had done, he and the others took a room each - and they began a fingertip search.

It was Kurt's job to search the kitchen, and the first thing he noticed was an unsavoury, slightly fetid odour. He screwed up his nose in disgust. Having to examine British people's rubbish was demeaning. He lifted the lid off the kitchen bin and the smell increased.

He pulled a face - but he knew he was on to something. He took the bin liner out and tipped the rubbish on to the kitchen floor. He picked over tomato-sogged toast crusts, congealed baked beans and pork bones, and found a carrier bag with the handles tied in a knot. He undid it and shook the contents out. A mass of crispy-looking brown hair tumbled on to the ground, followed by a used hair-lightening kit.

'Attenzion! Attenzion!' he shouted, and the other officials came running.

'Well, well, well,' said Athol, a bald man with a gap between his teeth. He was British, but he had been working for the Malvanians before the invasion. 'I think we have found what we were looking for.'

Athol took out a mobile phone and keyed in a number. As he did so, he told the female official to begin an examination of any computers in the house. Smiling, Kurt put the hair in one forensic bag and the hair dye kit in another. Athol took the evidence out to the car, and the search continued.

***

The front door at the Hardy's house had been kicked so hard that it lay halfway along the hallway. Jane's favourite houseplant had been knocked from the hall table, and a mixture of pink petals and soil had been trampled into the carpet by four pairs of shiny Malvanian army boots. The kitchen was a mess, and Doug sat on the floor, shoulder to shoulder with his wife, propped up against a kitchen cabinet. He was nursing a cut lip with a tea towel, and Jane was rubbing her ribs, one side of her face bearing a stinging red mark in the unmistakeable shape of a human hand. They were both too shocked to speak, and too frightened to move. There was a noise in the hallway, and Doug felt his stomach lurch. He pulled Jane towards the sanctuary of his chest in expectation of a second attack, but instead, Mr Jafary appeared at the kitchen door. His eyes were dewy, but he stood proudly and smiled. Then he produced a small packet of tea from his breast pocket and waved it at Doug.

'Those ruddy soldiers aren't so clever, you know,' he said. 'As you can see, my dears, they failed miserably to find my secret stash.'

Doug smiled as Mr Jafary picked the kettle up off the floor, filled it with water and plugged it in. He kissed Jane on the forehead and helped her to stand up.

'Now then. Biscuits,' he said.

***

The four officials completed their search of the Marshall's house. Kurt helped his female colleague load Lucy's computer into the boot of the car. Athol was on the phone again.

'There has been a lot of recent activity on one of the computers,' he said. 'It appears that the girl has used the search engine several times, but at this point her intention is unclear. We are bringing the computer in to HQ for further examination.'

The soldiers were making their way back to the van. Kurt noticed that one of them was hiding two bottles of Steve Marshall's whisky under his jacket. He smiled. He was sure he could persuade the soldier it was in his interests to share one of the bottles with him. He closed the side door of the van and gave the thieving soldier a knowing look. The van drove off. Shortly afterwards, the car carrying Kurt and his three colleagues sped off behind it. Kurt folded the sun visor down again and smirked at himself in the mirror.

The car screeched down the quiet street and disappeared round the corner on its return journey to London.

Chapter Thirty-Five
The Sweet Taste of Victory

Harold Stone was enjoying breakfast in bed in an expensive hotel. A whiff of smoked salmon and scrambled quail's eggs lingered in the room and croissant crumbs were scattered over the quilt. He burped. He wasn't used to rich food – Phyllis was far too stupid to cook anything so sophisticated. He downed his third glass of champagne and burped again. He picked up a small pot of caviar, emptied the whole thing on to a triangle of toast, smeared it around with a knife, pushed it into his mouth and swallowed it whole. Then he fingered a plate of pastries, finally settling on a sticky pain-au-chocolat. He patted his stomach as he ate - simultaneously eyeing a selection of smoked sausages on the top shelf of the breakfast trolley.

A telephone on the bedside table rang. The call was brief:

'A group of our officials have raided a house on ze outskirts of the M25. We have found evidence that ze girl has been there. We are on to her, Mr Stone.'

Harold put the receiver down and leapt out of bed.

He grabbed a fistful of pastrami slices in one hand and his underpants in the other. He got dressed, feeding himself with his free hand whenever he could. As he knotted his tie he tried to eat a Danish pastry without holding it, but he bit it in half and it fell on the floor. He combed his thinning hair in front of the mirror, and went into the bathroom. He rinsed out his mouth with spearmint mouthwash, then returned to the bedroom and picked up his jacket. As he hurried towards the door he trod on the half pastry that he had dropped, soiling the floor with a streak of French custard. A loud belch exploded between his lips and the hotel room door closed behind him.

Chapter Thirty-Six
The End

Hundreds of children filed out onto the school field in silence. They organised themselves into rows of twenty-five and turned to face the school building. On the direction of the Chief Instructor of Physical Education, they placed their right hand on the shoulder of the child next to them and shuffled sideways until everyone was an arm's length apart. Rousing music was played over a public address system, and everybody gave the salute of the Malvanian Youth. The music came to a triumphant halt, and the Chief Instructor shouted a new command:

'The Fundamental Creed and Affirming Promise of the Malvanian Youth Movement!'

Every child recited the Promise in Malvanian, their hands pressed to their hearts. Beth took out the card she was given in her Skoolpak at the first camp, and looked at the English translation:

'I acknowledge the supreme authority of the Malvanian Government.

The Malvanian Government is wise and great and good.

The Malvanian Nation must always be obeyed.

Our Malvanian fathers will provide us with everything we need.

I promise to live my life according to the Malvanian Way, for if we are loyal to our Malvanian fathers, then they will be loyal to us.

Those who stray from the Malvanian Way are to be pitied, and then re-educated.

For the Malvanian Nation shall be powerful and triumphant. For ever and ever, boundless and beyond.'

Their voices rang across the field and bounced off the walls of the school. Power and obedience oozed into the air and fed off each other like a parasite and its host. Beth looked around her in disgust. Could no-one remember what life was like before the Malvanians came and took their freedom away?

'At ease!' shouted the Chief Instructor.

Everybody relaxed.

'Prepare for Basic Aerobic Warm-up Exercises!'

Everyone straightened up again.

'And ONE! Two, Three, Four, and STRETCH! Two, Three, Four and STRETCH! Two, Three, Four, and DOWN! Two, Three, Four ...'

Beth looked along the row of children and saw a peculiar look of exhilaration on everybody's faces. She longed for Melissa to be at her side, pulling faces and making idiotic noises. But, instead, the girl who had cried herself to sleep last night was hopping and jumping next to her like a well-trained dog. She focused her mind on her escape plan, and prayed that Peter and Daniel would be ready.

The Chief Instructor barked another set of orders, and she threw herself into the exercises, pretending to be a model member of the Malvanian Youth.

Harold's bony fingers tightened on the steering wheel as he drove his old brown car through the gates of the school car park. His was the third vehicle in a convoy of four. In front of him were two black limousines owned by the Malvanian Government; behind him, a jeep carrying four soldiers.

He stopped the car. A woman called Valda Goög opened his door with a flourish and he got out. The soldiers joined the officials and the group stood for a moment, as hundreds of children, with their backs to the car park, exercised on the school field in rows of twenty-five.

'What a glorious sight,' said one of the officials.

The group made their way towards the school building. As they walked up the left hand side of the field, the Chief Instructor told the children to jog around the perimeter of the field. At his command, everybody turned to their right - and, once again, the children had their backs to the visitors. Row by row, the children set off round the field. With a posse of soldiers behind him, Harold held his head high. Unseen by the children, he followed the Malvanian officials along the path and through the door which led to the headmaster's office.

***

Forty minutes later Sammy was helping Beth get kitted out for her first game of *Flünken*. Beth put on her helmet and Sammy laughed.

'You look like you're from outer space,' she said.

Beth checked the coach was out of earshot. 'This helmet

is the latest in safety technology!' she said. 'Those foam discs can take your head off if you're not careful!'

'Yeah - somebody got their eye smashed out last week,' said Sammy. 'The eyeball landed on top of the disc. It looked like a custard cake with a cherry on top.'

Beth sniggered loudly and tried to think of another joke, but the coach appeared.

'Because you are ze new arrival, you must choose a squad for ze first session of *Flünken*,' he said.

Beth picked Sammy first - then Peter and, later, Daniel. The remaining children organised themselves as retrievers of stray discs, and the coach chose somebody to operate the disc-firing machine. The players arranged themselves in the correct formation, and the coach put his whistle between his teeth.

'Prepare to play!' he shouted. 'Three, two, one ...'

'*Haltzen!*'

The coach's whistle fell silently onto his chest, swinging on its ribbon.

'*Haltzen immediatzlich!*'

The headmaster, flanked by Malvanian officials and soldiers, was walking towards the playing area.

'Nobody move!' said the headmaster, and the four soldiers placed themselves around the group of children. Peter started sucking his thumb and twiddling with his fringe with the other hand. The most senior official spoke.

'Lucy Marshall step forward.'

Everybody watched Beth walk to the front of the group.

'Take your helmet off,' the senior official said. He turned to Mr Stone. 'Is this her?' he asked.

Stone had never looked more pleased to see someone.

'But you are not Lucy Marshall, are you?' the official continued. He paused to remove a speck of dirt from the sleeve of his suit. 'We have a traitor in our midst. An enemy of the Malvanian Nation.'

Two officials grabbed hold of Beth. Valda Goög picked Peter up, yanking him into the air by one arm. Beth screamed in rage and kicked Valda's shins.

'Behave yourself!' screeched Valda. 'Or your brother will feel ze wrath of ze Malvanian gun!'

A deathly hush descended over the field.

'Now,' said the official. 'Who can tell me ze third clause of ze Fundamental Creed and Affirming Promise of ze Malvanian Youth?'

Nobody raised their hand.

'Answer me!' he screamed.

'The Malvanian Nation will always stand firm and must always be obeyed,' said the girl who had cried herself to sleep the night before.

'Good. And ze sixth rule?'

A boy put his hand up.

'Those who stray from the Malvanian Way are to be pitied,' he began.

'AND?' said the official.

'And then be re-educated,' said the boy.

... But nobody heard him.

In the next street, an explosion shook the ground and sent a plume of flame rocketing upwards. There was a prolonged burst of distant gunfire. A second explosion followed about half a mile away, and then a third. The sky filled with the crackle of bullets, and the ground shook again and again as shells detonated across London.

'Our Malvanian colleagues are under attack!' roared the headmaster.

The soldiers ran off and everybody scattered, including Valda and the officials, who let go of Beth and Peter and ran for cover. A stray bomb ripped a hole in the ground at the edge of the school field, sending a fountain of earth and fence posts into the air, and one of the metal stakes catapulted, spinning, towards the school. Mr Stone ran after the senior Malvanian official and clutched the back of his suit. The official tried to shake him off but Stone gripped the fine cloth even harder. The fence post flew towards them, gliding elegantly across the sky. Then it fell, and – like a majestic heron seeking a fish – swooped low and embedded itself in Mr Stone's throat. He collapsed and dragged the Malvanian down with him. The official tried to crawl away - but Stone would not let go. The Malvanian struggled to his knees, unbuttoned his jacket and slithered his arms out of the sleeves. He shrugged Mr Stone's bleeding body onto the grass and, without a backward glance, he ran off towards the school.

Beth grasped Peter's hand and felt his fingers tighten around hers. Daniel was standing a couple of metres away, and she sprang towards him and grabbed him with her other hand. The noise of the shells was coming from everywhere at once. She filled her lungs.

'Run!' she yelled.

Chapter Thirty-Seven
Breaking Free

Beth pounded across the field towards the car park, dragging Peter and Daniel with her. Hundreds of pairs of frightened feet trampled the turf in all directions. Out in the street, the shelling intensified, each crash and bang punctuating the sound of children screaming and gasping in shock. Out of nowhere six British Army helicopters appeared low overhead, powering towards the centre of London, machine guns poised to destroy the enemy.

She reached the low fence that bordered the car park and heaved Peter and Daniel over the top of it. The boys stood, wide-eyed, waiting for her to climb down beside them. She snatched hold of their wrists and pulled them across the tarmac towards the convoy of vehicles that had arrived earlier.

There was a skirmish out in the street and a hail of bullets spewed into the car park. She dived behind one of the Malvanian limousines, drawing Peter and Daniel in towards her torso and shielding their heads with her arms. The bullets ricocheted off the armoured bodywork and bounced onto the ground like metal rain, and she realised that it would be impossible to break into such a heavily reinforced vehicle. The army jeep would be fast but it was open-topped, and they couldn't afford to be mistaken for Malvanian soldiers. There was only one option remaining: Mr Stone's battered old car would have to be their getaway vehicle.

The gunfire eased. Beth took hold of Peter and Daniel by the collars of their PE shirts and moved them to the rear of the limousine. She nodded towards Mr Stone's car.

'When I say go, we run as fast as we can, OK?'

A bullet shattered the windscreen on the jeep.

'*Go!*'

Doubled up, the three of them lunged towards the car and fell down beside it. Two hand grenades detonated in the street, sending a drizzle of mud onto the cars. The bullets stopped. British Resistance personnel ran away into the distance, their mission accomplished.

Beth inspected the front passenger window of the car.

'Wait here,' she said, 'I'll find something to smash it so we can get in.'

Peter tugged at her shirt.

'No!'

He was leaning against the rear passenger door that had the dent in it. He reached up to the handle, pulled it, and the door clicked open.

'Justin Baldwin showed me,' he said. 'We pretended to drive it when Mr Stone wasn't looking.'

Beth bundled the boys in through the back door and got in beside them. She climbed into the driver's seat, reached underneath the dashboard and pulled down a handful of wires. She selected two of them and yanked them hard so that they became dislodged. She twisted the exposed strands of copper together and the engine hummed into life. She glanced in the rear view mirror and looked at her passengers. Daniel was crying. Both boys were as pale as ghosts and seemed very small.

'It's going to be OK,' she said. 'You mustn't be afraid of the fighting – it's the good guys come to beat up the Malvanian bad guys, yeah? Now put your seatbelts on and hold tight.'

She put the car in gear and pressed her foot onto the accelerator. The engine stuttered.

'How come you know how to drive a car?' said Peter.

'Tell you later,' she said.

She turned hard on the wheel and they sped out through the car park gates and onto the road.

The streets surrounding the school were deserted, and she headed south at speed.

'We'll be home soon,' she said.

A fizzing sound cut through the air and a shell landed behind them. The force of the explosion caught the car and she lost control of the wheel. They careered off the road under a shower of shrapnel and came to rest in a hedge.

'Jeez,' she said. 'Everyone OK?'

She put the car into reverse gear. The engine screamed like a banshee and she drove backwards on to the road, then careered forward again in a cloud of exhaust fumes.

As they turned onto a high street, a supersonic roar boomed overhead. A trio of British fighter jets skimmed the rooftops on their way to the battle zone. Peter and Daniel twisted round in their seats to catch a glimpse of the aircraft, but they had already disappeared out of sight. They drove through a red light at a crossroads and turned left. As Beth steered round an abandoned checkpoint, a military lorry transporting Malvanian Army personnel turned into the same street. The lorry stopped and a dozen soldiers spilled out.

Beth turned into a side road on two wheels, a volley of gunfire piercing the shop walls behind them. She wove her way around the back streets, the Malvanian lorry in pursuit. A second wave of British jets flew in from the south and a single missile was despatched. The lorry erupted into flames, and blackened fragments of canvas fluttered down like funeral confetti.

'Don't look out of the back,' said Beth, and she motored onwards towards the outskirts of London.

Fifteen minutes later they were driving through the suburbs unchallenged. The air was clearer.

'Who was making all the bombs go off?' said Peter, peering out of the rear window again, and regarding the hazy cloud of dust and smoke far behind them.

Beth told him about the Resistance Movement, and how the British Army had been waiting abroad until the time was right to free Britain from the Malvanians.

'How come you know that?' he said.

'I was one of the Resistance.'

'Cool!'

She didn't want to talk about it. 'Do you like my very fashionable hairdo?' she said.

'You look like a pop star.'

She pulled up at a T-junction, then turned right onto a sharply sloping highway. A road sign said that the M25 was five miles away. Her navigation training was serving her well; they would soon be out in the countryside. They climbed upwards and rounded a corner just below the brow of the hill. The car struggled to maintain its speed as it neared the top.

'Anyone fancy a game of 'I Spy'?' she said.

'What's the matter with the car?' said Peter.

'It doesn't like the hill,' said Beth. 'Just you watch, though, when we fly down the other side!'

There was a shattering bang on the opposite side of the road. A house caught fire and disintegrated. A second shell exploded at the side of the road in front of them, and Beth swerved round the crater. A rocket seared past the side of the car and, after a few moments' delay, destroyed a van that they had driven past only seconds before. The car engine was making a banging noise and she cursed it for being so old and worn out. They chugged upwards and at last they emerged from the smoke and found themselves right at the top of the hill. Below them was the South East London Aerodrome, and on its runway the Malvanians were engaged in a fierce battle with the Resistance Movement to gain control of the airport. The Malvanians were barricaded into the airport buildings and were under artillery fire from all sides by a small band of Resistance fighters. The sudden appearance of an unidentified vehicle at the top of the hill did not go unnoticed. There was a lull in the conflict, as if both sides were staring at the car and weighing up what to do … and then, in the terrible confusion of war, both British and Malvanian forces took aim at Mr Stone's battered old car and attacked it with every weapon they had.

Chapter Thirty-Eight
No Way Out

'Get on the floor, both of you!' shouted Beth.

The two boys writhed out of their seatbelts and cowered between the front and back seats. Beth did a hand brake turn and the car spun round one hundred and eighty degrees, sending a foul-smelling vapour of burning rubber into the air. Peter and Daniel groaned behind her, the sudden movement turning their stomachs. She put the car into first gear and pushed the accelerator hard.

'Come *on!*' she begged, but the engine squealed and the car struggled to get back over the hill.

There was a bang immediately behind them and a rocket struck the road. The back wheels of the car jumped off the ground and the rear windscreen imploded, showering granules of glass over the back seat.

'*Go, go!*' she yelled, willing the car to pick up speed. But the accelerator pedal was already pressed to the floor. Another rocket landed just ahead of them, barely missing a street lamp, and the pavement crumbled as if it were made of pastry. Wisps of steam started to rise from under the bonnet of the car – and then, in a delayed reaction to the rocket strike, the street lamp toppled towards them. She changed up another gear and felt the car grip the road more firmly. She pressed the accelerator pedal again and this time the car responded. It moved forward strongly towards the top of the hill. With a dying creak, the street lamp collapsed onto the ground behind them like a metal tree and lay in the road, sparks crackling from its wire roots. The car reached the top of the hill and disappeared over the other side.

The sound of the conflict ebbed away. The downward slope gave the car momentum and Beth drove at seventy miles per hour, turning dangerously back into the T-junction they had emerged from earlier, and not stopping until she had put at least two miles between them and the airport. Then she brought the car to a halt with a jolt and leant forward, pressing her forehead on the steering wheel. Steam was streaming out from the engine in a continuous puff.

'Stupid, stupid, girl,' she said to herself. 'Some soldier you are.'

She closed her eyes. Commander Forsyth was right. She was a dumb kid who was playing at soldiers. How could she have driven straight towards the aerodrome? No decent soldier would have done something so idiotic. Her heart twisted as she remembered Ricky's words: 'I'm sick of being a babysitter ...' She had been so angry with him, but he had been right all along. She raised her head then brought it down on the steering wheel with force. It dispelled some of her frustration, so she did it again, and then again, rebuking herself with every hit:

'Stupid! - stupid! - useless! - ruddy! - stupid! - BABY!'

Her head felt as if it was going to burst.

'But you didn't have a map,' said Peter. His face appeared over the headrest. 'It's hard without a map. Daddy says. Don't be sad.'

She lunged round the seat and hugged him.

'You saved us,' said Peter. 'We think you're a brilliant soldier, don't we, Dan?'

Daniel's head popped up behind the front passenger seat.

'I want a wee,' he said.

When the steam had stopped pouring out of the front of the car, Beth opened the bonnet and unscrewed the radiator cap.

'We need water.'

She walked round to the back of the car and opened the boot. There was a large, half-full water container lying on its side at the back, the water inside frothy at the edges where the container had been thrown from side to side during the escape. Mr Stone had come on his journey prepared - and, just for a moment, Beth was grateful to him. There was also a selection of fruit in various stages of decay, where Stone had discarded Phyllis's efforts to give him something healthy to eat: two blackened bananas that were so old they had turned to liquid inside their skin; four dried and wrinkled apples, two shrunken satsumas and a paper bag which had once contained plums, which was now a soggy, bulging parcel with white mould sprouting on its surface. She picked up the water container and the two satsumas. She refilled the radiator and replaced the cap, then she pulled the skin off the satsumas and shared them with Peter and Daniel. The three of them sat on the grass verge by the side of the road, and sucked the lush juice out of each segment.

They were back on the road again. The car was driving more reluctantly after its struggle on the hill. But the M25 was not far, and they drove uninterrupted along leafy roads and past enormous houses that glowed in the sunshine. The road straightened and it became possible to see for a mile ahead. The air shimmered on the horizon, caused by the heat haze that was coming up off the tarmac. There was a series of distorted shapes dancing like flames in the distance, and Beth narrowed her eyes to try and make them out. As they got nearer, the hot air worked like a magnifying glass, and the rippled images straightened and expanded: it was a *Kantonlein* checkpoint building and half a dozen patrolling Malvanian soldiers. The men had spotted the car, and were grouping themselves to confront the vehicle.

The road they were travelling on had no turn-offs. It would look   suspicious if they suddenly went back the other way. Beth would have to approach the checkpoint and try to talk her way through, using the basic Malvanian she had learnt.

'You're going to have to hide on the floor again,' she said.

In the distance, the soldiers primed their weapons.

As the boys hid themselves her heart raced. She could feel sweat gathering on her top lip, and she sighed loudly in an attempt to calm herself. She drummed her fingers on the steering wheel as she approached the checkpoint and studied the positions of the soldiers. She could pull away at the last minute and smash through the barrier - even shoot the soldiers if she had to - but it would be a terrible risk. She slowed the car right down, allowing it to crawl forwards. The soldier in charge motioned with his hands that she should stop. Her stomach tightened and she slowed the car down as much as she dared, but still she inched towards the checkpoint. The soldier marched up to the car and looked inside. He spoke urgently to his fellow guards, gesturing to them to regroup. Beth thought she was going to vomit the satsuma pieces into her lap.

The soldiers withdrew their weapons. The barriers were opened and they were waved through, the soldier in charge saluting her as she passed. Beth returned the salute and increased the speed of the car, driving off down the road, watching in disbelief as the checkpoint got smaller in the rear view mirror.

'What happened?' said Peter.

'I don't know.'

As the *Kantonlein* disappeared from sight, she noticed that there was something stuck on the windscreen: a little picture of an eagle with a giant sword in its wings and the world at its feet. It was Mr Stone's Malvanian car permit.

Chapter Thirty-Nine
Homecoming

They drove on through country lanes, the sun streaming in through the windows, Peter and Daniel dozing on the back seat. The warm air lifted the scent out of the grass and flowers, and a light breeze carried the biscuity dust of the ripened wheat across the fields.

The car climbed a hill and the road became a concrete bridge. Beneath the bridge was the motorway that took traffic from the southeast coast into London. A convoy of British army vehicles was heading north, the Union Jack flying from every tank and jeep as the soldiers sped towards the capital. Behind them, a huge column of smoke was spreading across the sky from east to west and two fighter jets patrolled the skies. The vast formation of Malvanian tanks occupying the green belt had been blown out of the ground. Beth stopped the car and got out to watch the soldiers go past. She leant over the railings and, with the sun on her back, waved to the men below. They waved back, saluting in victory. At the rear of the convoy were two lorries flanked by military motorcycles. Beth ran across the bridge as the lorries passed underneath and watched as they came out the other side. They were full of Malvanian prisoners. She watched until their faces blurred into a single flash of pink, and returned to the car.

Peter and Daniel had woken up, and they blinked at her sleepily as she started the engine.

'You's two all right?' she said.

'I'm thirsty,' said Peter.

'Me too,' she said, 'but I think we should try and hold out until we get home, yeah? We don't want to bump into any stray Malvanians. It's not long now.'

She told them about the convoy of British soldiers and Peter looked disappointed.

'It's a shame Jackson didn't see them,' he said.

She felt as if someone had slapped her in the face. She'd forgotten about Jackson. She imagined him lying forgotten in Peter's dormitory, trodden underfoot in the panic and chaos, fraying and squashed and caked in grime - and it really upset her.

She drove on, blinking a teary mist from her eyes. Then her upper body started heaving uncontrollably and blubbering gasps erupted from her mouth. She had to stop the car. The engine died and she crumpled forward, sobbing. After all she had been through, it was the thought of a lost teddy bear that had finally broken her.

Five minutes later she became aware of herself again. There was something brushing against the back of her neck, and she turned round. Daniel was still buckled into his seat belt looking embarrassed, but Peter was leaning forward, one arm outstretched towards her. He was holding Jackson.

'He's trying to cheer you up,' said Peter. He withdrew the teddy and sniffed it. 'He's a bit dirty though.'

Beth let out another sob and waved at Jackson sheepishly.

'He was in my pocket,' said Peter. 'He was a bit scared of the fighting, but he wishes he'd seen the British soldiers, don't you, Jackson?'

She wiped another wave of tears from her eyes, blew her brother a kiss and apologised to Daniel for being an overemotional weirdo. Then she re-started the car. They were ten miles from home.

***

Doug and Jane Hardy were watching television. The British Resistance had taken over the BBC and was reporting on the progress of the uprising. Earlier that morning the street had been disturbed by gunfire, and a troupe of Malvanian soldiers was marched down the road in handcuffs by members of the British Army. At noon, the local radio station came back on air and said that the town was officially free. Doug was about to suggest an early lunch when a loud crash came from next door.

'Good God, what was that?' said Jane.

They hadn't seen Phyllis since Harold had driven off in a hurry just over a week ago.

'Get your shoes on,' said Doug, 'I'll grab the keys.'

***

Next door, Phyllis Stone was lying on the dining room floor, her face and arms mottled with purple bruises. By her left foot, a small, brown bottle lay on its side. It was empty; forty minutes earlier it had contained two weeks' supply of high-strength tranquilizers. Harold had punished her for begging him not to go to London, and now she needed to punish herself. She had grabbed hold of the Welsh dresser as she passed out, bringing it down with a bang and smashing a sixteen-place dinner service that had never been used. Her face was grey; her eyes closed.

A familiar noise outside caused her to regain consciousness a little. She dragged her body across the floor to the window. It was Harold's car. She pulled herself up to the height of the windowsill and looked out into the street. There it was - with the dent in the side where it had been hit by a motorbike. He was going to be cross with her; she hadn't made any dinner. Then the car door opened, and Beth Hardy emerged from the driver's seat. Phyllis's mouth curved upwards into a feeble smile.

'Good girl,' she said.

Her eyes closed and her arms went limp at the elbows. She slid down the wall like a rag doll and landed on the floor.

***

Beth let the boys out of the passenger door and turned around to see her parents hurrying out of the house and heading for next door. They stopped in their tracks. Her mum gasped as she breathed in, and squealed as she breathed out; then she raced up the front path.

'Oh my Lord, are you real?' she said. She scooped

Peter up in her arms, and as he rested his head on her shoulder she burst into tears.

'Come here, little Dan,' she said, and Daniel buried his face in her tummy. The two boys began talking at the same time, and her mum smiled and squeezed them tightly after every sentence they uttered, but didn't appear to be taking in a single word they said. Beth smiled and flung her arms around her, giving her a huge kiss, then ran to meet her dad, who was leaning against the doorframe and blowing his nose loudly. Beth launched herself into his embrace.

'Told you I'd bring him back,' she grinned, kissing him on the neck.

He took a long look at her, stroking her shoulders.

'I'm not sure about this blonde hair, madam,' he said. 'You've been completely irresponsible, you know that, don't you?'

'You won't tell me off, though,' she said. 'You never do.'

There was a cry from across the road.

'Happy, happy day!' shouted Mr Jafary, who was jumping up and down on the doorstep and waving his arms. Mrs Hill appeared at her living room window, waving a lace handkerchief and smiling.

'Welcome home, you lovely children!' sang Mr Jafary. 'And God save the Queen!'

Her mum set Peter down on the pavement and, with one arm around each of the boys, walked slowly towards the front door. Beth waved to Mr Jafary and followed her dad inside the house.

Chapter Forty
Order Out of Chaos

The Hardys and the Watsons sat in the living room eating pizza and watching the rolling news on the television. Beth had squeezed herself into the armchair next to her dad.

'You will tell me all about it, won't you?' he said quietly.

'Yup,' she said. 'But not today.'

The telephone rang. Her mum picked up the handset.

'That's odd,' she said, 'it says it's your mobile, Beth.'

'Don't answer it,' said her dad. He looked worried. 'It could be the Malvanian authorities. The uprising isn't over yet.'

'The Malvanians didn't have my phone,' said Beth. She took the handset and walked into the kitchen.

'Hello?'

'Beth … it's Ricky.'

A hot thrill shot through her body and the back of her neck smouldered.

'I know.' She leant against the kitchen worktop, listening to his breathing.

'You made it home then,' he said. 'I was worried about you. We all were.'

She remained silent. The last time she heard his voice he said he couldn't care less about her.

'Our mission was a success,' he said after a while. 'We disabled a key Malvanian base and forced a surrender. Then we pushed forwards towards London and liberated four villages. And we all made it – though Julie took a bullet in the arm and Wally got blasted when a grenade went off. He went deaf for a couple of hours, but he's OK now. They both are.'

She heard him sigh.

'But you're OK?' he said.

'I'm really good.'

'Yeah?'

'Yeah. I got my brother back!'

'Seriously? Wow - you are one clever little soldier girl!'

Her stomach twanged at this second compliment. That's not what he said before when he was arguing with his dad in the bunker.

'Listen,' he continued, 'I can't talk for long - Dad would kill me if he knew I'd got your phone.' There were voices in the background and a siren went off. 'I was hoping that once this was over we could meet up again.'

'Oh.' Her head was spinning.

'Call me?' he said. 'You know the number!'

'OK.'

The siren in the background got louder.

'Give my love to Julie,' said Beth.

'I will. Take care, little miss soldier girl.' He hung up.

She put the phone on the worktop and pushed it from side to side with her finger. Her reflection was visible in the glass door of one of the kitchen cabinets: both cheeks were fizzing pink. But they no longer burned with the excitement of hearing Ricky's voice. Her overwhelming feeling was that he had treated her badly, and she didn't like it. She poured herself a drink of water and pressed the glass to the side of her face to cool it down.

The door opened and Peter came in.

'Mummy said Dan and me can have crisps with our pizza.'

Beth grinned and reached into the top cupboard. She gave him the crisps and stroked his hair. With one bag in each hand he slipped his arms around her and cuddled her tightly.

'Was it the Malvanians on your phone?'

She shook her head.

'When I go to school I'm going to tell the whole class how you rescued me,' he said. 'No-one else has got a sister as brave as you. And when I grow up I'm going to join the army and then I can do rescues!'

'So you don't mind telling other people you love me?' asked Beth.

'Of course not.' He wriggled free. 'Who was it on the phone?' He looked at her earnestly. He had dried tomato sauce on his chin and a bit of cheese in his hair.

'Someone who's less of a man than you are,' she said.

Peter left the kitchen. Through a gap between the doors of the serving hatch, Beth watched him jump onto the sofa in the living room and share the crisps with Daniel. She folded her arms across her chest and hugged herself and, as she did, she felt something in her breast pocket. She dug her hand in and pulled out the daisy that Ricky had given her. It had shrivelled into a desiccated wisp. She twirled the dried-up stalk between her forefinger and thumb. For a few seconds she remembered the spicy scent of Ricky's skin when he leaned across the front seat of the Land Rover and caressed her arm with the petals. She could smell all of it: the mud and the grass, the exhaust fumes, the plasticky whiff of the seats and the dusky fragrance rising from the pollen as the flower took on the warmth of her fingers. Then she remembered Ricky's petulant defiance of his feelings for her on the night she ran away from the bunker and the images evaporated. She walked across the kitchen and dropped the withered daisy into the bin.

'Grow up - and get lost,' she said, and the bin lid slammed shut.

She washed her hands and, as she turned away from the sink to reach for a tea towel, she was surprised to see her dad standing by the kitchen table.

'Didn't you hear the doorbell?' he said. 'Melissa's here.'

Her friend stood in the doorway, white-faced. Beth skipped to greet her and they hugged.

'Oh God, I'm so sorry,' said Melissa, tears growing in the corners of her eyes. She had never looked so careworn. 'What was I thinking? They could have killed you.'

'I'm fine,' said Beth.

'No thanks to me and my big mouth … I thought I'd never see you again.'

'Look at me – I'm OK! You should come and join us for pizza.'

Melissa seemed troubled. 'I'm not sure.' She cast a

wary look at Beth's dad: 'Has Jane forgiven me yet?'

He smiled apologetically. 'That might take a wee while.'

'Am I missing something?' asked Beth.

'Your mum paid Melissa a visit,' said her dad. 'After we read your note. I'm afraid she rather blames Melissa for everything.'

Melissa dug her hands into her pockets and looked at the floor. 'I thought she was going to strangle me. I gave her all that stuff about 'parents always want what their kids want'. She told me it was crap.'

Mum did? This was impressive, thought Beth.

Melissa hugged her again. 'Oh God! My idiot days are over. I promise.'

'Come on, let's eat before it's all gone.'

They walked into the living room. Her mum nodded at Melissa to acknowledge her presence, and made a curt gesture that she should join the party.

'I must go and check on Phyllis in a minute,' she said. 'I'd forgotten about her in all the excitement.' She looked at Melissa coldly. 'Some of you have a lot of catching up to do, I'm sure.'

Mrs Watson offered Melissa a slice of pizza. Beth had never seen her friend look so uncomfortable.

On the TV the newsreader announced that the Royal Family had been reinstated. They showed the Queen getting out of a Land Rover and said that Her Majesty would be giving a speech at three o'clock to declare that Britain was, once again, run by the British. A reporter said that the Prime Minister had been liberated from the Malvanian Parliament - but had immediately been arrested for treason. There was a short film showing the Prime Minister being pushed into a windowless van by British police. The van drove off at great speed and hurtled round a corner.

'I hope he gets travel sick,' said Beth.

The pictures of the Queen in her Land Rover were shown again.

'Got any champagne?' said Mr Watson.

'No champagne …' her dad got out of the armchair and walked towards the door. 'But we do have a bottle of fizz somewhere.'

He disappeared and returned with a plastic bottle full of bright blue liquid. Peter and Daniel immediately looked interested.

'I thought I'd told you to throw that away,' said her mum.

'Well, it's all we've got,' said her dad. 'And I think it calls for the best glasses – come on, Beth.'

After Beth returned from the kitchen the drink was poured into a set of expensive crystal goblets. Mr Watson sniffed it and screwed up his nose.

'What the heck's this got in it?' he said.

Her dad looked at the label. 'Don't ask,' he said. He lifted his glass. 'To the future!'

Everybody raised their glasses, and on the television screen the people of Britain began to party in the streets. The two families drank the blue liquid and, as Mr Jafary led a conga line of pensioners along the pavement outside the window, they all agreed that it actually tasted very good indeed.

THE END

Acknowledgements

Louise Voss, for constant support, constructive editing and kind feedback. Mike Oldfield-Marsh for technical support and being the best baby brother ever. Diane Reddish for telling me about Louise's writing course at Kingston Uni. My wonderful team of young readers who gave fabulous feedback early on: Amelia, Isabella, Freya, Eva, Elisabeth, Rebecca, Emily, Abigail, Josie and Helena.

And to all you other super family and friends who have given kind advice and support when I needed it: you know who you are. Thank you.

Want more adventure, friendship and fun?
Go to **www.fionabeddowbooks.com** for news, articles, interviews and writer's secrets.
And Beth Hardy is on Facebook!
Search for '**Beth Hardy Fierce Resistance**'
and see what she is doing right now.
Fiona Beddow is on Twitter : **@FionaBeddow**
Fierce Resistance has its own Facebook page, too!
facebook.com/FionaBeddowBooks

WHAT'S NEXT?

A new heroine, a new mission ...
another girl stretched to her limits.
Fiona Beddow's second breathtakingly fast,
heartstring-pulling adventure is darker and more
dramatic than the first.

The J.A.S.M.I.N.E. Portfolio

ON SALE FROM THE END OF 2014...